SPECIAL DELIVERY

By
KRIS NEVILLE

I0541488

ARMCHAIR FICTION
PO Box 4369, Medford, Oregon 97504

For more information about Armchair Books and products, visit our website at…

www.armchairfiction.com

Or email us at…

armchairfiction@yahoo.com

THE IMMINENT INVASION OF EARTH!

Over thousands of years, the Knoug System had been strong in its belief that "There are the Rulers" and "There are the Ruled." Unfortunately, during the passage of those countless generations, the Knoug had transformed into an evil and power-hungry civilization. Now, the Knoug Empire was ready to capture a planet…then destroy a whole System! Unfortunately for mankind, the planet in their cross hairs was Earth—a world that the Knougs considered to be the next target in their on-going interplanetary campaign against their hated intergalactic nemesis, the Oholos.

Parr came to Earth as one of the first Advanceman for the Knoug invasion. His mission: to set in motion the process that would demoralize the whole planet just before the invasion…

FOR A COMPLETE SECOND NOVEL, TURN TO PAGE 101

CAST OF CHARACTERS

PARR
Advanceman for the alien Knoug system. His job was to demoralize the people of Earth prior to a massive invasion from space.

LAURI
An "Oholo" who had hopes of trying to prevent an interplanetary war and played a pivotal role in saving the whole planet!

BERTI
A simian-like earthman hired by Kal to eliminate two Oholos who were getting too close.

KAL
He had savage eyes, even with his Earthling disguise. Could he help Parr escape the Oholos?

HICKLE
An innocent Earthling hired by Parr to send out "paperwork" that was paramount in the Knougs' invasion plans.

CHAPTER ONE

A CANNONADE of shellfire met the silver listening post as it zipped across the moonlit desert. It twisted erratically, trying to dodge. Then a radar controlled gun chuckled to itself, and the listening post faltered in flight, slipped air, plunged sandward.

In the Advanceship, far above and to the west, one of the Knougs pressed a button and the listening post exploded in a white flare.

Afterwards, no fragments could be found. The newspapers said the usual thing. The government issued the usual profession of disbelief—and finally even the gunner became convinced of the usual explanation: he had tried to pot Venus.

While on the Advanceship the Knougs continued to prepare for D-Day.

CHAPTER TWO

THREE days later, on D-Day minus thirty, the Advanceship began to move eastward, seeding down advancemen toward strategic centers in North America.

Towns with big post offices.

And then on over the Atlantic toward other continents.

Parr was the first advanceman to land. The coat tails of his conservative double breasted suit fluttered gently as he fell; air, streaming by, fretted his hair. Except for the anti-grav pack strapped to his back, he could easily have been mistaken in a more probable setting for an Earthman.

5

Parr came to Earth as the advance guard for an invasion. His mission: to see that every person received a package that was being mailed—

SPECIAL DELIVERY

By

Kris Neville

Minutes later his feet touched the ground with scarcely a jolt. He peeled out of the anti-grav pack, pushed the button on its disintegrator time fuse and dropped the pack. He lit a cigar and blew smoke toward the cold bright stars.

He walked from the weedy lot to the nearest bus stop. No one else was waiting. Darkness had concealed his descent. He sat down, stared stolidly at the darkened filling station on the opposite corner.

When he was halfway through the cigar the Los Angeles Red Bus came by and he stood up, boarded it, fumbled in his pocket for change.

"Thirty cents, buddy," the driver said.

Still holding the cigar, Parr counted out two dimes and two nickels. He tried to hand the driver the coins, which were excellent imitations, as was his suit, his cigar, and all the rest of the Earth articles.

"Put it in the box, buddy."

Parr obeyed.

"Hey," the driver said as Parr turned. "Your check." The driver held out a strip of red paper.

Parr took it.

"No smokin' on the bus, buddy."

Parr dropped the cigar and mashed it out. He shuffled down the aisle, sank into a seat and half closed his eyes.

Furtively, then, he began to study the occupants—his first near-at-hand contact with the natives. At the same time he tried to form a mental liaison with some of the other advancemen.

For a moment he thought he had one to the east, but there was a hazy swirl of interdiction that erased all contact.

ABANDONING further attempts he tried to search out the frequencies of the minds about him. Once he managed to touch a series of thoughts innocently concerned with household details and with an overtone of mild and nameless anxiety. Aside from that he received nothing except the din of electronic impressions at the extreme lower end of his range.

He half-turned to stare out of the window. The passing landscape was peaceful in starshine and the buildings stood proudly defenseless. In imagination he saw the illuminated, "You'll—take—a—shine—to—this—fine—wine" sign hanging askew over a backdrop of smoking rubble. And it was delicious to know that this would be fit and proper.

Although the preliminary intelligence report (based on nearly four years of preparatory scouting) contained no instance of Oholo activity on the planet, he listened, high up, on their frequencies, (particularly here, vulnerably near their own system it would be no fun fighting them.) He let his shoulders slump with relief, let the smile of satisfaction come.

As reported, the frequencies were clear: Earth was, indeed, their blind flank.

He closed his eyes, relaxed completely, took quite a joy in the knowledge that shortly Earth would be the lethal dagger pointed at the heart of the Oholo system.

At the Beverly Hills transfer—for Hollywood-the-film-capital-of-the-world—Station, two drunks boarded the bus and settled in the rear, singing mournfully.

Parr grew increasingly irritated by the delay. When the bus finally started, making the sharp turn from the lot and throwing his body to the right against the steel ledge of the window, he cursed under his breath.

The dismal singing went on. It picked up telepathic overtones, and Parr gritted his teeth trying to block out the bubbling confusion that scattered from the drunken brain. He opened and closed his fists. Anger flared at him: the anger of impotence. For a moment, he dared to imagine the planet contaminated, the population quietly dead, the Knougs working from sheath hangers. Only for a second; but the brief thought was satisfying, even as he forced himself to agree with the strategy of the War Committee: which was to leave the planet as nearly un-poisoned as possible by even a minor land war.

Finally the song bubbled to silence. Half an hour later the bus turned on Olive Street and the gloomy Los Angeles buildings hovered at the sidewalks. It pulled in at the Olive Street entrance of the Hill Street Terminal and Parr got out.

He walked out of the lot and started downhill toward the Biltmore Hotel.

WHEN Parr awoke he knew that something had been added to Los Angeles during the night. He shivered involuntarily and tightened his thoughts down to the place where no fuzzy, side harmonics were possible.

He was afraid—the startled afraidness of finding something deadly underfoot. Gradually he made his body relax; gradually he quieted his twin hearts; gradually he corralled his breathing. Then he let out a wisp of thought as tenuous as mist.

And he sensed the Oholo's mind again. Very near to his own. He closed his mind quickly, waited breathlessly to see if the Oholo had detected him: His ears hummed with danger for he was within mental assault range.

There was no answering probe and after a moment he got up cautiously.

Feeling the rug beneath his bare feet made him wince with a blind associational terror, which he could not immediately analyze. Then, looking down, he thought of the tickle of Tarro fur. He half expected to see the dark stains on the rug too. Always, on Tarro fur—remembering—there were those stains. They had been a difficult people to rule. As *agent provocateur,* (that had been several years ago on Quelta) he had reason to expect blood.

He crossed to the trousers neatly folded over a chair. In the left front pocket was the comset. He fumbled it out and standing naked in the gloomy dawn, whispered: "Parr. There is an Oholo in my hotel."

After a pause the comset issued the tinny question: "Is he aware of you?" The voice filtering through the small diaphragm was without personality.

"I don't think so."

There was silence. Then: "Is he open?"

"I think…he is, yes."

"Find out for sure!"

The comset was cold in Parr's hand. He stood shivering. He rubbed his left hand over his naked flank.

HE tried to kill his thoughts against the command from the Advanceship, tried to let the drilled in obedience take over. He opened the receptive portion of his mind as far as it would go, knowing that within seconds seepage would be as loud as thunder because he was not adept at double concentration. But even before one second had gone he snapped his mind closed again.

The Oholo was open.

"Parr," he whispered hoarsely into the comset. "He's open."

"...He can't know we're here, then. What did you learn?"

Parr mopped his forehead with the back of his hairy arm. "I just kept receptive a second."

"Keep checking, then."

Parr let the comset fall to the chair. He walked to the window and looked out at the haze bound city. Early sunlight fought blue smog. Across the street the Pershing Square pigeons waddled self-consciously about on the grass beside the new fountain, picking at invisible tidbits and cooing.

Parr rubbed his throat trying to massage away the inner tenseness. He was alone against the Oholo. An aloneness that he had not been prepared for. And he worried at the fear that was inside him.

He dressed with awkward fingers and left the room, his eyes darting suspiciously along the corridor as he drew the door closed behind him.

He walked quickly down the carpeted stairs and through the front doors of the hotel. Several times he glanced over his shoulder as he hurried toward Sixth Street.

After four blocks he was sure that he had not been followed. He entered a restaurant. He ordered, reading from the menu.

He did not enjoy the meal.

AFTER eating he took a cab to the office of R. O. "Bob" Lucas, Realtor. The Advanceship had determined that Lucas was the agent for an empty warehouse on Flower Street.

Parr exposed a bulky wallet for Lucas' benefit and began to rustle bills with blunt, stubby fingers. Within minutes he had signed a six-month lease.

After making an appointment for three o'clock Tuesday at the warehouse, Parr left Lucas' office and caught a cab to a typewriter shop. He purchased a Smith-Corona portable, a ream of corrasable paper, a disk eraser, and five hundred business envelopes. At the bookstore next door, he bought a United States Atlas.

After that he took a cab to the post office, had the driver wait while he rented six postal boxes under the name A. Parr and bought twenty sheets of air mail stamps.

In the cab once more, he concentrated on the city map that had been impressed electronically on his brain. "Drive out Sixth Street," he ordered, being very careful of his enunciation.

A half dozen blocks out Sixth, Parr located a hotel on the right side of the street. It was a reasonably safe distance from the Biltmore. He ordered the driver to stop.

The building sat atop a hill, the street before it twining briskly toward the center of town. Parr studied the building for a moment, memorizing details of architecture for reference.

Then settled with his purchases in a front room on the 3rd floor, Parr opened the Atlas to the Western United States and marked out the territory assigned to him with the heavy ink lines of his pen.

Having done that, he listed all the names of the included towns.

Then he sat down at the portable, inserted a sheet of paper and wrote:

"To the Chamber of Commerce, Azusa, California. Gentlemen: Please send me the current city directory." He looked at the postal numbers. "My mailing address is..." He typed in the first number on the list. "...Los Angeles, California. Enclosed is five dollars to defray the costs. Thanking you in advance, A. Parr."

HE studied the letter. It was a competent job of typing. He flexed his fingers, found them slightly stiff from the unaccustomed work.

He ran his eyes down the list of towns, inserted another sheet of paper.

"To the Chamber of Commerce..."

He stopped typing.

He sat before the typewriter imagining the number of directories, imagining the staggering total of individual names.

He thought of the Advanceship and its baffling array of machines that would automatically scan the directories and print a mailing label for each of the names. He thought of the vast number of parcels waiting to be labeled, as many as fuel requirements permitted the Ship to carry. And of the even vaster number that the synthesizer was adding out of the native resources. The smooth efficiency of the Advanceship, the split second timing of the whole operation... And all of it auxiliary timing to the main effort. Even with superior weapons, even with complete surprise, the Knougs were taking no chances. The job of the Advanceship, the job of Parr, was to demoralize the whole planet just before the invasion. To insure an already certain victory.

He turned back to the typewriter, wrote a few more words.

There was still the awareness of the enemy Oholo in the back of his mind.

He split the list of cities into six equal groups for box numbering.

Several hours later another tenant complained about the noise of the typewriter. Parr gave the clerk fifty dollars and continued to type.

CHAPTER THREE

PARR spent the morning of Tuesday, D-Day minus 28, in his hotel room, reliving what seemed now to be the extremely narrow escape of the previous morning. He imagined what he *might* have done: assaulted the Oholo mentally, or struck him down with the focus pistol when he tried to leave the hotel. And having imagined the situations he proceeded to explain to himself why, instead, he had fled.

At eleven o'clock, by prior arrangement, he reported to the Ship and from it received the reassuring information that the now alerted advancemen had been able to find no other Oholo.

At noon he went out to eat and then for an hour walked the streets, studying the people and their city. Most particularly he listened for accent, intonation. He was afraid to drop his mind shield to try for telepathic contact with them.

A few minutes before three o'clock in the afternoon his cab drew up to the warehouse. The air was hot and sour smelling and Parr was restless. The realtor was waiting for him on the sidewalk. Parr nodded curtly. The man bent clumsily and rattled keys at the lock.

"Here it is," Lucas said.

Parr walked into the warehouse.

It was an old building. Perhaps shabbier, dustier than he had expected. The air was stale and faintly chilly with decay. Remnants of packing crates, wrapping paper, labels and twine had been heaped in a greasy pile in a far corner.

Parr sniffed suspiciously as his eyes darted around the room.

Across from him, above the rubbish, an electric box indicated that the building had at one time been industrialized at least to the extent of a few heavy power tools.

Parr walked to the stairway.

"I'll want someone to clean this mess up," he said curtly.

"Yes, sir," the realtor said.

"Tomorrow," Parr said.

"All right," the realtor said, consciously omitting the "Sir" as if to reassert his own individuality.

Parr glanced at him. "I'll send you sufficient money to cover the fee." Without waiting for an answer, he started up the stairway.

The upper two floors were in much the same condition as the first. From the third there was a narrow flight of steps slanting to the roof. Parr eyed it with disapproval.

"Narrow," he said.

"There's seldom any reason to go up there…sir."

PARR went up. At the top of the flight, he forced back the door and clambered into the shed, which opened onto the roof. Parr dusted his knees. He stepped outside, and the gravelly finish grated under his shoes. The air smelled of warmed over tar.

He tugged restlessly at his chin. It was a good, substantial roof. As the listening post had reported. Good enough for pickup and delivery. He permitted himself a glimmer of satisfaction.

He heard movement behind him. Instinctively he whirled around, his hand dipping toward his right coat pocket, the memory of the Oholo the vision of a composite Oholo face surprisingly like an Earth face—flashed across his mind. The realtor's head bobbed into view, and Parr relaxed his tense muscles.

"How is it up to here?"

Parr rumbled an annoyed and indistinct answer and turned once more to the roof. When the realtor stood at his side, Parr said, "I want that shed thing ripped off and a chute installed, next to the stairs. Have it done tomorrow."

"I'm…" the realtor began. But he looked at Parr's face and licked his lips nervously. "Yes, sir," he said after a moment. "Anything I can do. Glad to oblige."

"That's what I thought," Parr said, and Lucas shifted uneasily.

Parr turned to the stairs. Going down he could see dust motes flicker in the fading light at the dirty west windows.

Outside he watched the realtor lock the doors.

"Keep the keys," Parr said. "Send them to me at the Saint Paul Thursday morning. At eight o'clock."

The realtor said, "…Yes, sir."

AT six o'clock Parr was in his hotel, undressed, making preliminary arrangements by telephone to hire a fleet of trucks. He had already placed an advertisement for shipping clerks and common laborers in *The Times*: interviews Thursday from ten to four at the Flower Street warehouse.

After finishing with the truckers, he phoned four furniture companies before he found one open. He ordered it to deliver a desk and two dozen folding chairs to the Flower Street warehouse Thursday morning at nine-thirty.

All the while the Oholo was in the back of his mind, now sharp with sudden memory, now dull with continued awareness.

He checked the schedule the Ship had given him.

He took the comset, flicked it on. "Parr. I'm scheduling. I'll need a packet of money along with the dummy bundle. Can you deliver them both to the warehouse tomorrow night?"

"We can."

"Good," Parr said, swallowing, and there was perspiration on his upper lip.

"Have you contacted the Oholo again?"

He felt his blood spurt. "Not yet," he said.

He waited.

Then: "Think you can handle him mentally?"

Parr glanced at the mirror, saw how taut his reflection was. "I'm not very sure," he said.

"Well, physically, then?"

Parr let out his breath slowly. "I don't know."

"Try. Either way. Get rid of him. An Oholo could cause the invasion trouble."

Parr plucked nervously at his leg. "If I'm not able to?"

The comset was silent for a moment. Then the impersonal voice said, "If you are killed in the attempt, we will replace you." It paused for a reply. Receiving none it continued: "Get what information you can, even at the risk of exposure. It's too late now for them to mount a defense, and they probably have no way to alert the natives. We want to know what he's doing there, and if there are any more on the planet."

"All right," Parr said, and he realized, gratefully, that, to the Ship, his voice would sound emotionless.

He dropped the comset. His hand was shaking.

Not so damned good. How to kill the Oholo?

HE tried to steady his nerves by remembering other planets, other times. He had faced danger before, and he was still alive. Except that before the danger had never been an Oholo. He had been Occupation, not Combat. He remembered the few captured Oholos he had seen. They died slowly when they wanted to be stubborn.

Finally he crossed to the bed and stretched out naked, relaxing slowly, knowing that the time had come to get what information he could. Muscle by muscle he began to go limp.

Slowly, very slowly, he dissolved his mind shield. When it was completely gone he began to inch out, to flutter out, concentrating with all his power a stream of receptive thought on the Oholo frequencies high up and uncomfortably shrill.

He located the mind, far away, and he began to skirt in toward it, his own mind trembling in anticipation of the blow if he were detected.

He inched closer trying to make himself, completely non-transmitive. He could feel seepage around the beam, and he shunted it to a lower frequency, holding it there, suppressed. The effort blunted his full concentration and when he finally began to get Oholo thoughts they were blurred. He picked up a scrap here, a scrap there, his body tense.

When he relaxed at last, forming his shield solidly, he was weak. He held the shield desperately, chinking it against a possible attack. None came. The Oholo was still completely unsuspecting, completely lulled by the security of its environment.

Feeling a sense of elation and a new confidence, Parr went to the comset. "Parr. Oholo report."

"Go ahead."

Parr concentrated on the wording, filling in the blank spots with his mind. Abruptly he was aware of an inadequacy, something elusive that he should be able to add. He wrinkled his face, annoyed. But the uncertainty refused to resolve itself into words. "His name is Lauri. He's here on a mission having to do with the natives. I got no details, but it doesn't directly concern us, I'm sure of that. There appear to be several more on the planet. They seem to avoid cities, which accounts for the fact that advancemen haven't reported them." For a moment, he almost placed his thoughts on the elusiveness, but again it escaped him. He paused, puzzled.

"We'll have the advancemen warned. This may be damned inconvenient, Parr. If there are many of them."

"I couldn't get the exact number without exploring his mind. If I'd done that, I might not have been able to report afterwards."

"Go on."

"He's leaving the city in a few days. You still want…me to try to kill him?"

"Yes."

The Oholo, Parr could not help remembering, had as strong a mind as he had ever encountered.

WEDNESDAY morning Parr walked to the Biltmore, not hurrying, not anxious to face a free and dangerous Oholo.

At the side of the hotel he risked contact. A shutter movement of thought told him the quarry was still inside the building.

He crossed Olive at Fifth with the light and angled right into Pershing Square. He located a seat from which he could observe the entrance of the Biltmore. For one moment he considered mental assault; but remembering how strong the mind was he faced he discarded that course.

He waited. He walked around the Square. The morning seemed endless.

Finally he risked another shutter of thought.

The Oholo was still there.

Noon.

He ate in a drugstore across the street.

Still there.

As the afternoon wore on, the weariness of waiting left his body and the success of the shutter contact inflamed him with confidence. He could cross the street, enter the hotel, seek out the room. But he delayed—without admitting to himself that he was still afraid.

The gloom in the air was pre-sunset, city gloom, nostalgic. He consciously dilated his pupils to accommodate the fading light, unaware now of the scurry of people on the sidewalks and the roar of the city cloaking for night amusement. Neon lights came on like cheap fire, out of the darkness, infinitely lonely.

He shifted uncomfortably. He stood up. He could wait no longer.

Then a man and woman emerged from the hotel. And he tensed. A wisp of thought, unsuspicious, floated to him on mental laughter.

The Oholo, Lauri.

He shielded his mind even tighter, scarcely thinking.

He began to amble in the direction the couple were taking, keeping to the opposite side of the street.

At Sixth they turned toward him, waited through the yellow for the green light. They crossed.

He paused studying a Community Chest sign, his hearts pounding uncertainly. He felt a curious little probe of thought that was delicate and apologetic, as if reluctant to intrude upon anyone's privacy. It passed him by undetecting.

THE man bent toward the girl, a pert blonde, and laughed in answer to something she had said. Parr watched them go by and then at a short distance swung in behind them. He touched the focus weapon in his right hand pocket, a crystal-like disk with one side tapering to a central point. It was a short-range weapon, palm aimed, fired with an equally exerted pressure on the lateral sides.

Even with his mind closed Parr could catch ripples of Oholo thought: amusement, sympathy, appreciation. For a moment he was afraid that he had been mistaken somehow, for again there was the elusiveness, an unreality he could not account for in terms of the situation.

Parr narrowed the gap between himself and his prey.

And they turned a corner. Parr crossed the street, drew still closer, in time to hear the girl say, laughing, "...slumming once before I go back." The crowd thickened and Parr found himself sidestepping passersby. He was almost near enough, and his hand was moist on the focus gun.

The couple turned into a cellar nightclub. Parr swore to himself. Taking a nervous breath, he descended the steps. He nodded to the bouncer-doorman who was leaning idly against the wall.

He stepped into the nightclub. He saw the man help the girl to a table.

Parr brought out his hand. His eyes were suddenly hot and beady with excitement.

On the far side of the room he saw the black lettered sign, "MEN." He would, in crossing to it, pass directly by the Oholo's table.

As he began to move forward a woman stumbled unsteadily against him, knocking him off balance.

"Whynacha watch where ye're goin', ya...," she began shrilly, but, with his left hand, he brushed her out of his way. She took a half step backwards, undecided.

He turned to glare at her and under his gaze she looked away and tugged nervously at her dress.

Parr walked swiftly toward the rest room, his every energy concentrated on his mind shield.

As he passed the table, the girl shuffled uneasily on the chair.

Without breaking stride, Parr fired the focus gun into the man's back.

He was clear of the tables when he heard, from behind, the initial surprised, "Oh!"

He had one hand on the door marked "MEN" when he felt the confusion in his mind. Automatically, he pushed open the door. A puzzling realization that something was wrong…

He turned left, from the narrow corridor into the rest room proper.

And he went down to his hands and knees on the filthy tile, writhing in agony.

CHAPTER FOUR

THE hurt, mostly, was in his brain, and he choked back a scream. He could not think. And then the outer edge of the shield began to crumble.

He concentrated. Every muscle, bone, nerve. Veins stood out on his neck. He fought.

He was dented by fire inside his head. Hot, lancing tongues of flame. He tried to shrink away. He whimpered, groveled. His hands fumbled uselessly.

She was nearly inside of him now. It was almost over. Her thoughts were like fingers rending and tearing at quivering unprotected flesh.

He struggled hopelessly, retreating under a mental assault of unendurable ferocity. His outer memory was ripped away, a section of his childhood vanished forever.

And then there was desperation in the assault wave. He could feel her trying to shake off an attempt to breach her concentration. He stiffened, relaxed, arched his body, struggled with her.

Her attack suddenly crumbled into a distracted muddle. Her concentration had been shattered.

His mind was trembling jelly, creamed with throbbing pain. But he could resist now, and slowly he forced her out.

"I'll be back!" she lashed at him. And the hate in the thought was alive. "I'll kill you for this!" Then her thoughts began slowly to fade away and her mind shield came down.

Parr shook with every muscle.

"Buddy. Buddy," someone was saying, shaking his shoulder. "You sick, huh?"

He struggled to his knee twisting his head back and forth, trying to regroup his memories. The sear places were vacant, empty, part of himself cut cleanly away. Immediate memories not yet stored and filed seemed to be floating free, unassociated—too widely spread to have been cut out, not too widely spread to have been mixed and shuffled. He was panting as he struggled with them, capturing them, tying them down, ordering them.

Then he began to vomit.

"You drink too much? Hey, buddy, you drink too much? I guess you drink too much, maybe?"

UNDERSTANDING—half-understanding—came with the words. He scrabbled up the wall until he was erect. His back pressed against the vertical tile for support. He turned and staggered from the stinking rest room, his hands forcing clumsily against the walls.

In the short hallway he could hear voices.

"And when he slumped over..."

"She just sat there like she was *thinking*..."

"You see the cop shake her?"

"I thought she was gonna hit him with the ashtray."

"Well, they sure hauled her outta here!"

Parr staggered back into the nightclub. Eyes turned to stare at him. His head spun in nausea. He began to move leadenly toward the exit.

There was a police officer in his path.

The officer reached out to stop him, and he tried to shake the hand away from his shoulder. He tried to think, to reactivate his trained responses, knowing that he would have trouble with this man.

He muttered wordlessly. The officer looked grim.

"Not drunk," Parr gasped. "Sick."

The officer was incredulous.

Parr shook his head, and an explanation appeared from the basic psychology of the natives: a coded scrap, death-fear.

"It...it...was horrible seeing him like that."

The officer hesitated.

"One minute he was alive, the next minute..."

"Yeah. Yeah. You better get a cab, buddy."

"Fresh air. I'll be all right, with fresh air."

Suddenly sympathetic, the officer helped him up the stairs.

Once outside the wave of sickness began to recede. Parr waited unsteadily while the officer signaled for a cab.

As he got in the cab he whispered, "Drive."

The driver looked suspiciously at his fare, but the policeman said, "He's sick, that's all. He's just sick."

The driver grunted, meshed gears.

"Where to, Mister?"

"Just drive," Parr said tonelessly, rolling down the window until he felt air hitting his face. He lay back against the seat cushions.

BALLOON-like, memories floated, rose, fell. He struggled with them. Drifting away, his hotel's name. Before he lost it, he bent forward, muttered it at the driver.

The Oholo—a female, he knew now—suddenly whispered in his mind from a distance: "You killed the wrong one, didn't you?" He struggled with his mind shield in terror, finally got it set against her. He shivered.

At the hotel, he stumbled from the cab, started in.

"Hey, Mister, what about me?"

"Eh?"

"Money, Mister. Come on, pay up!"

He fumbled at his wallet, found a bill, handed it over.

In his room at last, he peeled off his suit, his underclothes.

He lay prone on the coverlet.

After hours, or what seemed hours, his mind was stable enough for hate.

He lay in the darkness hating her. Even above the instinctive fear he hated her.

He tossed in fever thinking of after the invasion when she would be captured. The last of the sickness ebbed away. His thoughts adjusted, found more and more stability.

Slowly he drifted toward sleep, which would heal up the confusions. As he hovered in the dark of near sleep, he felt a wash of mental assault from too far away to be effective. Her thoughts tapped at his shield and he dissolved it partly to let a little defiance flash out.

"I'll get you!" she answered coldly.

And after that, he slept, healing.

HE awoke, automatically assessing the damage. It was less than he had expected. Sleep had resolved it into tiny confused compartments.

And he knew how hard it would be to keep up his shield for four weeks. There was fatigue on it already.

Then, too, there was the pressure. A gentle insistent pressure. As if to say, "I'm here." He remembered how strong Lauri's mind was and he knew that she would be able to hold the pressure longer than he could hold the shield. Once, in training he had shielded for nearly thirteen days—but now, under the sapping of his energy by physical activity, by the multiple administrative problems, by the pressure itself…

He shook his head savagely.

He looked at his suit across the edge of the bed. He shuddered with the memory of his sickness and reached for the phone to order new clothing.

And the pressure. He was going to have to learn to get used to it.

Later, he reported to the Ship, his voice fumbling and hesitant.

The answer crackled back. "She's alerted the others, you idiot! We picked up her message. There's four more of them down there."

Parr tried to think of an excuse, knowing how pointless it would be even to offer one.

"You should have used your head," the Ship continued. "What made you think the Oholo was necessarily male?"

"I…I don't know. I just did."

"You know what happened on Zelta when an advanceman was careless? You want that to happen here?"

"I…"

On Zelta? He knew it should be familiar to him. He cursed inwardly, reaching for other memories, to see how many he had lost… A sentence, unbidden, flashed across his mind: "Never sell an Oholo short." It was what someone had told him once. "They think differently than you do." How, he pondered confusedly, could they expect him to think like an Oholo?

"I can't think like an Oholo," he said tonelessly.

"You could... Never mind."

"I could? Listen, how can they be thinking, to leave a flank like this unprotected? Why didn't they take this planet into protective custody long ago? How can you *think* like that? They aren't logical. How could I know they'd let a woman..."

"Parr!" the Ship ordered sharply.

Parr gulped. "Sorry."

"Insubordination on your record."

Parr clicked off the comset.

Damn! he thought angrily.

There was still the annoying pressure on his mind. "Damn you!" he thought without lowering his shield. "Damn you!" he thought again, dissolving enough of the shield to let the thought escape.

She did not answer.

There was a knock at the door.

A man with his suit.

IT was almost ten o'clock when Parr arrived at the warehouse. The windows were alive with sunshine, and through them he could see the freshly cleaned interior.

The men with the furniture were waiting, the driver angry at the delay, his assistant indifferent. Already there was a line of job applicants who shifted uneasily, eyes turned curiously upon Parr as he crossed and unlocked the warehouse doors.

Parr, one hand resting on the knob, said to the deliveryman, "Bring the stuff inside."

The driver growled and picked up a clip board from the seat. "I gotta bill here, doc. You wanna pay before I haul the stuff out?" He held out the clipboard, jerking it savagely for Parr's attention.

Parr glanced at the sum. He reached for his wallet. One by one he removed the bills and handed them over to the driver. When he had met the amount there were only two bills remaining.

"Now take them inside."

"Okay, doc."

Parr went immediately to the roof. The shed had been knocked down as he had ordered, and the chute had been installed.

The two packages were lying at the top of the chute. The bundle of money and the sample, dummy parcel—both night deposited from the Ship. He picked them up.

Walking down the stairs, he peeled away the wrapper from one bundle, exposing green sheaves of currency. Back on the ground floor he put the stacks of bills on the newly arrived desk, and the dummy parcel in the drawer. He took one of the chairs, carried it to the desk and sat down.

He looked toward the door.

"You, there! At the head of the line! Come here." He was careful of his accent, realizing the necessity of impressing the waiting workers. He was pleased to find the accent near perfect.

The woman, frail and elderly came forward hesitantly. "My name is Anne, sir."

"All right," he said, reaching for a bill from the top sheaf. "I forgot to bring a pen and paper. Take this and go get some. You may keep the change, and there'll be another bill when you get back."

Her eyes widened. "Yes, sir." She held out a wrinkled hand.

He did not need to glance toward the door again to know that an initial and important impression had been established.

After she had gone, Parr leaned back in the chair and said to the other applicants, "You may come in now."

They shuffled inside.

PARR watched them settle into chairs. As he did so, he was aware of *her*, Lauri, holding the pressure steady on his mind, and memories of last night came back. Concentrating away from them he tried to analyze his feelings toward the natives. He found a mixture of contempt and indifference.

"I'm going to say this only once," he announced crisply. "I will expect you to inform any late comers. When I have finished I will interview each of you."

He balanced his hands before him on the rim of the desk, holding them steady. He looked around at the waiting faces. He let his mind relax, and the speech—it had been graven on his brain in the Ship—came bubbling to the surface. He searched forward along it, and he found it to be complete, untouched by his contact with the Oholo. He wrinkled his forehead and began, seeking to give the impression that each word was being carefully considered.

"I intend to hire some of you to help me sort and load packages of promotional literature. Those hired will be paid five dollars an hour."

They shuffled unbelievingly. "Yeah, but when, Mister?"

Parr's mind dipped for information. "Whenever you wish to. At the beginning of every day. Will that be satisfactory?"

The listeners twisted uncomfortably, embarrassed by their doubt. "Now you're talkin'," the original critic said.

Parr cleared his throat heavily for effect. "The work day may be as long as fourteen hours, depending on the circumstances."

No questions, now.

"The literature will come already packaged and labeled. It will be delivered to the roof by helicopter, and your job will be to sort it and transfer it to trucks." He looked them over. "I will need you for approximately three weeks."

The pressure was still on his mind, not demanding, merely present. He writhed at it inwardly. Outwardly he was calm, his voice undisturbed.

"Hey, Mister," another of them said. "I'd like to get somethin' straight right now. You ain't havin' us to handle no explosives or somethin' dangerous like that, are you?"

It was an objection Parr had been prepared for. Scarcely thinking, he bent to the drawer and picked up the dummy parcel. He put it on the desktop.

"There is no danger. You will need no special instructions save to handle as you would normal mail. I have a sample package here." He bent over and stripped off a section of wrapping paper to permit them to see a stack of printed material.

HE rippled the dummy sheets with his thumb. "The nature of the advertising is secret for the moment, but," he lied, "this is what it looks like." He returned the bundle to the desk. "It's just paper." That was true, and he smiled faintly as he imagined the amount of disorganization mere paper would be able to accomplish. For an instant, the uncertain emotion returned as he thought of the invasion fleet, rushing communicationless through hyperspace for its rendezvous with Earth.

"There is, of course, a reason for the high wages," he said, the words coming automatically. "We want to hit the market before—ah—" and the phrase and the hesitation were memorized, calculated for effect, "a competitor."

He pursed his lips speculatively. "Naturally we want to avoid publicity. Anyone violating this requirement will be dismissed immediately."

He seemed to study the faces individually, looking for spies from the rival company. I will probably not require you for more than a few hours the first several days. In that event, you will receive pay for a full eight hour day."

He stopped talking, and the applicants' faces were excited.

"As soon as the woman returns with the paper, I will begin the interviews. Those of you whom I hire will receive a fifty dollar bonus before you leave the building."

When she returned, Parr interviewed. His questions were perfunctory. By noon, he had enough workers, and he had one of them hang out a penciled sign reading: "Jobs Filled." After that, he closed the doors and assembled them before him.

"If you'll form a line, I'll give you your bonuses. Give me your names to check against my list. You will sign a sheet or paper here in receipt. I've hired enough people to take care of any of you who do not choose to come back tomorrow, so there will be no further vacancies and no chance to collect a second bonus... Report for work at nine o'clock tomorrow morning. At that time, I'll have someone here to fill out the necessary government employment forms for each of you."

Sitting at his desk, he began to count out the bills into neat little stacks. After each applicant had signed, he pushed a stack toward him.

After that he spent the afternoon making further arrangements with truckers and locating a woman to handle the employment records of his workers. He even had time to purchase some extra clothing and buy a few personal articles.

As night fell, while he lay comfortably naked on his hotel bed, he felt the pressure on his mind begin to fluctuate subtly.

CHAPTER FIVE

THE Oholo, Lauri. Strong minded, yes. But untrained.

And realizing this, Parr smiled, for it testified to the certainty of his superiority, a superiority he should have recognized from the beginning. He was dealing with an amateur, an Oholo who had never received even the most elementary instruction in individual tactics.

What she was doing now was glaringly obvious to a professional: cruising the town in an attempt to locate him. But in contacting his shield by focusing the pressure, directionally, she failed to realize that the space variations would not only tell her of his location but also inform him of her movements.

Cautiously Parr began the defensive procedure. Step by step he engaged the pressure with his mind, rather than letting it rest on his shield. Then he began to counteract the distance pulsations—strengthening, weakening, presenting a continual pressure against her questing thoughts, compensating for her movements.

But in a very short time she realized what had happened. She altered the pressure sharply. A split second later he joined it again. The advantage was still his. She altered once more. He followed suit. Check.

He could almost feel her angry confusion. Then after a moment she let the pressure fall into a rhythmic pattern. A lullaby of monotony that was the result of concentration rather than of the distance variations. He knew what to expect and after fifteen minutes it happened. She broke the rhythm suddenly and tried to plunge inward, to center on him before he could counter. He had not been lulled, however, and she accomplished nothing. He met the assault easily.

The rhythmic pattern returned. Every few minutes she broke the pattern and tried to plunge in again. But his mental screen absorbed the shock.

She was persistent.

Finally Parr grew weary of it—then vaguely annoyed—then exasperated.

When he was thoroughly uncomfortable she tried another swift change of tactics. She began to increase the pressure, slowly, inexorably—stronger and stronger against his defense. He blocked her, held, retreated, held again, keeping the shield in readiness. Shortly, perspiration stood on his forehead. Abandoning the defensive he fought back against her.

But she blocked him; they locked in a deadly mental tension of spiraling energy that weakened Parr with each passing second.

SHE held the tension longer than he would have thought possible. And when it eased, it vanished, leaving his mind uncontacted. Instead of relaxing, he formed his shielding, expecting a sudden assault.

None came. Instead, the gentle insistent pressure returned, undiminished by her efforts. She was stationary now; the pressure was steady.

His body had been tense for a long time. It ached, and he was physically exhausted. His hand shook a little as he brushed at his leg, waiting for the space variations to begin again.

They did not.

But the initial confidence—generated by the realization of her inexperience—was no longer so bright.

The very pressure itself now was an emotional drain and he wanted to lower the mind shield and relax completely. But even at a distance a mental assault would sting like a slap, like a cut, like disinfectant in a raw wound.

Under the strain, sleep was lost. Instead there was uneasiness.

He tried to ignore it. He forced himself to remember his home village. It had been a long time since he had thought of it, and at first it was difficult. But after a while, memories began to open up with nostalgia: the clumsy citizens with their mute opposition to the Empire, a *jehi* farmer who had once addressed his class on planetism and afterwards been shot, the smell of the air, the look in people's eyes, night...the stars...

The stars were cold and bright and far away. Imposing symbols of Empire.

His mind turned comfortingly on that, and his planet seemed dwarfed and unimportant. The Empire, with its glittering capital system, the sleek trade arteries...the purposeful masses of citizens...the strength and power of it, the essential rightness of it. Something you could feel in the air about you and smell and see. It was a thing to be believed in, to be lost in, to surrender yourself to.

It was strong, crushing opposition, rolling magnificently down the stream of time—splintering, shattering, destroying, absorbing, growing hungry and eternal. He was part of it, and its strength protected him. It was stronger than everything. There could be no doubt about Empire.

But a single Oholo was strong, too.

He stirred restlessly on the bed, unable to dissect out the thing that bothered him when he thought of the Empire. His thoughts had run the full cycle, and they were back where they had started.

It seemed for a moment as if his mind were a shiny polished surface, like an egg floating beneath his skull, hanging on invisible threads of sensation that ran to the outside world.

The room was full of moonlight.

WITH fascination he studied the wallpaper, a flower design scrawled repetitiously between slightly diagonal lines of blue. He concentrated on the rough texture of the paper, let his eyes drift down to where the paper met the cream siding, revealing twin rifts of plaster. A thin line of chalk-like dust had fallen on the wood of the floor. The edge of the rug, futilely stretching for contact with the wall, curled fuzzily.

A faint breeze fluttered the half-drawn blinds, puffed the lace curtains, rippled in to his bed and body.

He was guilty of something.

He wrinkled his face, puzzled.

What was he guilty of?

No answer, and the moon went behind a cloud, bringing depression and acute loneliness, sharp and bitter. A depression bleak in its namelessness, and terrifying.

Then suddenly his mind jerked away from the thoughts.

He realized he was not countering the Oholo's movements. The steady pressure was a compensated pressure, varying as her distance. A projection requiring mental ability he could never hope to equal. She had learned fast. She had neatly sidestepped his defense. Terrified, he probed beyond his shield, and for an instant received an impression of her distance. He sat upright, shivering. She had worked much nearer. In desperation, he launched an assault, closing his eyes, forgetting everything else.

Lightly she parried him and slapped back strongly enough to make him wince.

Then for two long hours they fought. He grappled with the pressure, working on the theory that it was a burden no mind could carry indefinitely.

But she did not concede. Instead she continued, giving up trying to come closer, intent on breaking down his will to resist. He checked her with all his energy. He countered, stared at the scattered moonlight on the rug.

Energy drained from him until he wanted to scream, to plead with her. And beyond the bleak reality of con-centration he knew that she was using twice as much energy as he was.

Then she began to weaken. The pressure steadied, and he could feel her exhaustion. She was through for the night.

The sheets of the bed were damp. His body trembled. He wanted to whimper pathetically in fancied defeat.

Sleep slowly came, and the long pervasive influence of Empire, the influence visible in concrete form on conquered planets, swept over him.

But somehow he was guilty of something, he knew...

HE was still tired when he awoke, instantly alert, wary. She apparently still slept, although she held the pressure against his mind.

Dawn ushered in a cloudy day, and street noises—cars, trolleys, movement—came into the room with the utmost clarity.

He would have to change hotels. That alone had an urgency to it. Wearily he fumbled with his shield. It was still solid. He ran a hand over his forehead, pressing against the temples.

He thought of the sleeping Oholo.

He dropped the shield completely, knowing she would realize its absence. He stretched mentally for a long, precious second, and it was with infinite relief.

"Hello," he leered in the direction of Lauri. "Hello," he snarled suddenly, tingling with excitement.

No answer.

"Hello! Hello! Hello!"

He shielded, and hatred of her and of all Oholos—inbred hate, overcame him. It brought an almost pathological bravado with it. The destructive drive for revenge was a surge within him. He dropped the shield and thought to her, slow and gloatingly, of the things in store for her when she was safely disarmed and helpless. And he permitted his hate to leap and caress her, and the details of the torture were etched in passion acid.

After a while, he could feel her shudder at the thoughts, and he simpered. She seemed to lie helpless, stunned under him, spurring him to greater imaginative excesses.

Then she struck out blindly, a shivering blow that caught him unaware between the eyes like a swung club.

HE shielded. Instantly he felt the guilt of last night. He was angry with himself, as if he had acted without really wanting to, as a Knoug was supposed to act. And he snarled a curse.

The maddening, uncompromising pressure returned. Implacable. Patient. Unanswerable. Pressure that would drive him insane if he had no eventual hope of release. He shuddered, and the sense of depression—the night sense— was even more dark and terrible in daylight.

He got out of bed, reported to the Advanceship, keeping his voice low and even.

"Parr. Scheduling."

"Check."

The voice from the Ship was a stabbing, accusing voice. A voice that *knew*, that had made, overnight, a secret and awful discovery about him. He wanted to grovel before it and plead for forgiveness...

Nonsense!

He licked his lips nervously. "That damned female!" he shrieked.

"Eh?"

"That damned female, don't you see!"

"Parr, what's wrong? Listen, Parr, are you all right down there?"

Suddenly he relaxed. "Nothing. Nothing's wrong."

"Are you sure?"

"Yes," he said. "I'm just a little nervous."

HE ordered the driver to stop. The building was columned, red brick, decayed. The sidewalk before it was grimy, littered, cracked, chipped. Listlessly, people shuffled down the street, flecks from the vortex of humanity farther uptown drifting in the backwater of the city. Faded overalls, jeans, thin unpressed cheap suits, frayed shirts and crumpled soggy collars. Faces—lean, hollow, blotched; eyes that were harried, red, tired. The women, still trying to retain the snap of movement, were like wind-up toys, almost run down.

Parr grunted at the smells of the area, and straightening up to pay the driver, noticed distastefully the slack faces, defeated eyes and shuffling steps.

Then he knew: here, pressing in from all sides was reassurance. He watched a haggard face, felt pity, shook off the emotion as unworthy but still felt it. He could understand the haggard face. But distaste returned again, for he was superior to the face. He blocked off his mind, refusing to consider the natives any longer...

He took a room inside the dingy, wasted building. He hung his extra suit in the closet. The wall was greyish with cracking plaster and water stains, half hidden by the dim light; the rug underfoot was threadbare and stale. On the dresser, a Gideon Bible, nearly new.

The sheets, he discovered upon turning back the bed, were dingy and yellowish. The mattress sagged in the middle and the metal bedstead was chipped and dented.

After he was settled he reported to the Advanceship, told of his new location and the reason for it.

On his way out of the hotel he was conscious of the guilt again, and in the street, he stopped an old man who wore a tobacco stained shirt and gave him several of the bills from his wallet. Bribing helplessness made him feel better.

Back in the hotel that evening, renewed confidence came as he thought how clever he had been to choose such a location; he thought of the Oholo searching across town, her mind automatically rejecting this location. It would take her more than one night to find him.

But her mind did not seek contact with his; instead, the pressure remained annoyingly general.

She was making no attempt to locate him.

He stared out the window at the pale reflection of neon from the sidewalk. She was not even moving yet.

He waited, suddenly nervous.

When she finally began to move she still kept the pressure general.

He checked her position and after an instant met opposition that scattered his thoughts. But in that space of contact he knew she had moved closer.

In terror he drew his shield in tight.

SUSPENSE mounted in his mind. He counted his pulse beats, quieting himself. He tried to relax. Then fearfully checked her position again. That involved receiving a sharp slap of assault, for she had been ready with an almost trigger response.

And she was closer. She seemed to be advancing confidently.

In nervous haste he began to dress.

And then she struck with her full hellish power from very near at hand.

Amazement and fear flamed in his mind. He fought to strengthen the shield. She forced it back, got a single hot tentacle of thought through into his mind proper, and it lashed about like a living thing before he could force it out.

Gradually he came to realize that she was not near enough for the kill.

He staggered to the door, his mind numbed and spinning as if a giant explosion had gone off by his ear.

And then, somehow, he was in the street, half dressed. Somehow he managed to find a cab. It was all a blur to him that might have taken two minutes, five minutes, or twenty minutes. She had abandoned the assault. She was moving closer.

Then, before the cab began to move he saw her. Two blocks away: Coming toward him. Her face was impassive, but even at a distance, the eyes…or was it his imagination? The focus gun…in his pocket… The cab drew away. He leaned out the window, twisting back, tried to aim at her. The shot, silent and lethal, sped away. The distance was too great.

Then a new assault, but it was too late. He held it until the cab outdistanced it. She renewed the pressure and he could think again. And he knew, in the back of his mind, that soon now they would meet. And he shuddered, wondering of the outcome.

HE was sick. Unbelievably, she had outguessed him. She had guessed he would flee away from the obvious to the other extreme.

His breathing was hoarse and painful, and he thought comfortingly of his home planet; a small planet with a low sky; incredibly blue, a trading station far removed from Earth, satisfyingly deep in the Empire. As a boy he had often gone to the spaceport to watch the ships. He remembered how he had stood watching their silvery beauty and their naked violence. He had always been very excited by them. Always. And they were a symbol of Empire.

After the cab driver had spoken to him several times he roused himself to say, "A hotel, any hotel."

It was luck he knew, that he had been beyond effective range. She might have guessed the correct slum hotel and stood below his window.

His mind was foggy and befuddled.

And he had been hurt. Much more than mentally hurt. More than physically hurt. He wanted to hurt something in return. Only now he was too tired.

He relaxed in the seat, listened to the hiss of tires. He would be able to sleep tonight. She could not figure out his next move, predicted on random selection.

In his new hotel room he found that his body stung and itched.

And she began to search for him. He had to fight her for more than an hour, and after that he slept, subconsciously keeping his shield on a delicate balance.

CHAPTER SIX

THE next day Parr went first to the post office and from there immediately to the warehouse. He brought with him three manila envelopes containing three city directories, the first responses to his requests. He took them to the roof, checked the three cities off his list, placed the directories at the base of the chute. Later the helicopter would come swishing down from the night sky, collect them, and return tomorrow evening with the compressed and labeled parcels, one to a family, stamped with the requisite postage. The parcels, spilling out of the compressor, would expand to a huge jumbled heap for the natives to handle. And Parr knew he was only one of many advancemen. The cargos would nightly spew to all points of the Earth from the Advanceship slowly circling the globe behind the sun.

Complete coverage was what the Knougs were aiming at. Here advancemen were using the government postal system for distribution; there, making arrangements for private delivery; elsewhere, setting up booths. Earth had been scouted very thoroughly by four prior Intelligence expeditions. It was an inconceivably complex network of planning, possible only through extreme specialization in an organization made frictionless by obedience.

THAT night Lauri's pressure increased—or seemed to—and he shook his head like a hooked fish. He began to walk faster, mumbling under his breath.

The solution, he knew, was distance. A partial solution only, for he was bound by assignment to commuting range, not great enough to permit him to lose her completely.

The jangle and clank of a city train roused him. An interurban trolley. It was stopped at the next corner accepting passengers.

He turned and ran the quarter block to board it.

As he rode toward the ocean he could feel the gradual lessening of the pressure; it was a lessening not nearly as pronounced as he would have felt were she trying to center on him as he fled, but sufficient to relax him. He could feel a puzzled pressure shift after a few miles as she checked him briefly, then an over excessive spurt of questing thought, which he countered automatically. Even if he only remained shielded it would take her at least a week to localize him except in a very general direction.

He began to feel all of the over-charged tenseness drain out of his muscles. He even began to take an interest again in his surroundings, studying the buildings with appreciation. The incongruity of the architecture was more apparent than before, due to his greater acquaintance with the thought patterns of the natives.

A bizarre sight: a temple in the style of the Spanish, low-roofed, unpretentious, comfortingly utilitarian with no nonsense except for the gleaming gold minaret atop it, its coiled surface outlined with neon tubing.

It drifted away, behind.

Here a huddled shop, antique-filled and sedate, less than a block from a brilliant drive-in in disk form, radially extending like a somnolent spider.

And most paradoxical of all, the false glamour of signs encouraging the spectator to rub shoulders with excitement that was supposed to be inside the door, but wasn't. For people who were incapable of finding it anywhere. Parr felt suddenly sad.

Odd natives, he thought. But even odder thoughts for a Knoug, he knew. Then he felt the savage stirrings inside of him again. It brushed away sadness. The numbered days until the invasion excited him. The emotional surge of danger and trial and obedience were the preludes to the necessary relief. Parr felt fully relaxed.

HE got off the trolley in Santa Monica, where the night fog as already fingering in from the ocean.

He crossed the wide street, angled toward the Mira Mar hotel.

In his room he stood looking out across the street over the stretch of park that broke suddenly as a dull clift, dropping jaggedly to the road beneath. Beyond were buildings unusually small and squalid in sea perspective. The beach, curving north to Malibu; and the sea itself was overshadowed toward the Ocean Park Pier by the brazen glitter of red neon.

But the fog was quieting the scene, and isolating it. After a bit there was no world beyond the window but the grey damp world of fog.

Still the excitement beat at him. He projected his thoughts beyond the immediate future to the bright burning of the

Oholo System, the atomic prairie fire skipping from sun to sun at the core, leaving the planets ashes—while isolated, the periphery worlds would one by one capitulate to Knoug power, to Knoug *will*, and become infected with Destiny.

Beyond that?

The doubt came, and he cringed mentally.

He was guilty of something.

His hands whitened on the sill, and staring into the fog he tried to bring all of the weight of Empire to his support.

But there was the memory of revolt by Knougs themselves on a tiny, distant moon.

The depression came back.

…It took the Oholo four nights to locate him.

CHAPTER SEVEN

THE strain on his face—the heaviness of his eyes—the taut lines of his throat. His body was exhausted.

Like dripping water the pressure pounded at him.

The night before, she had found him at Long Beach.

He cast off the depression to find euphoria; and the two alternated steadily with increasing peaks.

His hands were nervous. Blunt thumbs constantly scrubbed blunt fingertips in despair or anticipation… The trucking had all been arranged for.

The deliveries from the Ship occurred nightly. He had sent follow-up letters to cities that had not responded to his first request. The answers had finally arrived.

The warehouse, floor by floor, was filling. Already some trucks were waiting.

There was the continual bump of handled packages sliding from the chute, being sorted, being stacked. But worries piled up inside of him: fears of an accident, a broken package, a suspicious employee, a fire… The Oholo, the guilt, the depression.

Eagerly now he listened to the general information report from the Ship. Most advancemen were on schedule. No irreparable accidents. Certain inaccessible areas had been written off. A few advancemen recalled for necessary Ship duty. One killed, replaced, in Germany. World coverage estimated at better than seventy per cent in industrial and near industrial areas, a coverage probably exceeding the effective minimum—short only of the impossible goal.

He had been talking to a trucker in front of him without really hearing his own words, his fingers and thumbs rubbing in increased tempo.

He hated the man as he hated everyone in the building, everyone on the planet.

The trucker shrugged. "I'll have to deadhead back. That has to go in the bill, too."

"All right," Parr snapped irritably. "Now, listen. This is the most important thing. Each of the lots has to be mailed at the proper time. Your bonus is conditional on that."

"Okay," the trucker said.

"I can't overstress the importance of that," Parr said. He handed the slip of paper across the table. It was a list of mailing information, Ship compiled, that was designed to assure that the packages would all be distributed by the mails as near simultaneously as possible.

"You deliver the Seattle lot, that's number, ah, eighteen on the list, the last."

"I understand."

"When your trucks are loaded, you may leave. I'll pay you for lay-over time."

"I've got a bill here," the trucker said.

The two huddled over it, and after the trucker had gone Parr leaned back staring at the ceiling, his nerves quivering.

HE knew what he was guilty of, at last. Knowledge came suddenly, from nowhere like an electric shock, and it stunned him. Logically he demanded proof; but there was no proof. It came, it was; it was beyond logic. Nothing in his memory…and for a moment he thought he had lost the memory under Lauri's first vicious assault ripping into his mind; but, and again without reason, he knew it was not in the memory she had destroyed. She was connected with it, but not like that… He was guilty of treason. He could not remember the act, but he was guilty. What? When? Why? He did not know; he was guilty without knowing what the treason was: only the overpowering certainty of his guilt. Wearily he let his head droop. Treason…

"Mister Parr?"

"Eh? Eh?"

"There's somethin' heavy in this one. It don't feel like paper. I think it's metal of some sort. Now, look Mister Parr, I don't want to get tied up with somethin' that's not square. You said all these packages had paper in them. And I'd kinda like to see what else there is in this one, Mister Parr, if you don't mind."

Parr wanted to jump out of the seat and smash at the man's face. But he forced himself to relax.

"You want to open the package, is that it?" he said, gritting his teeth.

"Yes, Mister Parr."

"…Then go ahead and open it." Having expected refusal, the worker hesitated.

"Go ahead," Parr insisted. He kept his face expressionless, although, beneath desktop level, his hands bundled into knobby fists, white at the knuckles.

Then at the last possible second, as the worker's fingers were fumbling at the wrapping, Parr leaned forward. "Wait a minute. It won't be necessary to waste the parcel... Unless you insist."

The worker looked at Parr uncomfortably.

A question of timing. Events hung in a delicate balance between exposure and safety. Parr reached for the drawer of the desk, his movements almost too indifferently slow.

His hand fumbled inside the drawer. "I think I have some of the metal samples around here," he said. His hand found the stack of gleaming dummy disks, encircled it possessively. He tossed them carelessly on the desktop and one rolled, wobbling, to the edge and fell to the floor.

PUZZLED, the worker bent to the one that had fallen, picked it up, turned it over in his hand, studying it curiously.

"I don't see..." he said suspiciously.

"That's our product," Parr lied. "We include some in every hundred or so bundles. The literature explains their function."

The worker shook his head slowly.

"As you can see," Parr persisted gently, "they're perfectly harmless." He tensed, waiting.

"...Yeah, uh...I think I get it. Something like them hollow cement bricks they use to cure people of rheumatism with, huh?"

Parr swallowed and relaxed. "That's the general idea. You'll see... Well, if you want to, go ahead and open the parcel."

"Naaah," the man said foolishly. "...There wouldn't be no sense in doin' that."

Beneath the desktop again, his hands coiled and flexed in anger and hatred. "I want your name," Parr said, a very slight note of harshness in his voice.

The worker let his eyes turn to the backs of his heavy hands, guiltily. "Look, Mister Parr, I didn't mean..."

Parr silenced him with an overdrawn gesture. "No, no," he said, his voice normal and conciliatory. "I meant, we might be able to use a man like you in our big plant in the East." He snarled inwardly at himself for the unnecessary note of harshness before: it was too soon for that. Suddenly stammering with excitement, the worker said, "My name's George...George Hickle...George Hickle, Mister Parr. I got good letters from back home about my workin', sir."

"Where do you live, George?"

"Out on Bixel... Just up from Wilshire, you know, where..."

"I meant the number of the house, George."

"Oh." George told him.

Parr wrote it down. "George Hickle, uh-huh."

"I'll be mighty obliged, Mister Parr, if you'll keep me in mind."

"Yes. Well. Good afternoon, Hickle. You ought to be getting back to your work now, hadn't you?"

And when the worker had half crossed the room, Parr drew a heavy, black line through the name. He had memorized it.

The pencil lead broke under the pressure.

And at that moment, the pressure in his mind vanished.

In automatic relief, he relaxed his shielding for the first time in what seemed years, and before he could rectify the error Lauri hit him with everything she had, catching him just as the shield began to reform.

PAIN roared in his mind. From the force of the blow he knew that she must be near the warehouse.

It had been one quick thrust, leaving his mind throbbing and he sobbed in impotent hate and anger.

The pressure was back.

And slowly and surely she was closing in on him, compensating. She had struck prematurely, realized her mistake, and was narrowing the range, holding the final assault until assured of victory.

He stood up weakly and hurried to the door, brushing through a group of startled workers.

Outside, a cab was cruising, and Parr ran after it. It did not stop. He turned and ran frantically in the opposite direction, rounded the corner, still running, his heels thudding on the hot pavement.

He ran for blocks, the blood pounding in his head, sweat trickling into his eyes. Pedestrians turned to stare, looking back along his line of flight.

When Parr stopped, finally, he was trembling. He stared at his own hands curiously, and then he looked around him.

He swallowed hard. The world swam, steadied. His chest rose and fell desperately...

At the airport, he phoned the warehouse.

"Hickle? Get me Hickle... Hello, Hickle, this is Parr. Listen, Hickle, are you listening? Hickle, I've got to leave town for two days. You've got to run things. You understand? Listen. I've left money in the drawer of my desk...for the pay roll... You know how to run things, don't you, Hickle? ...Now, listen, Hickle, there's some trucking...wait a minute... Look... You stay down there. Right there. I'll phone you back, long distance, later. Don't go away, Hickle. Wait right there. I'll tell you what you've got to do."

The last call for his plane came over the loudspeaker.

"Listen, Hickle, I've got to run. I'll phone you later, so wait. Wait right there, Hickle!"

OVER Bakersfield, gratefully—infinitely gratefully—he felt the last wisp of pressure vanish.

He was free.

There was no consequence powerful enough to keep him from dropping his mind shield entirely. But he let it come down slowly, barrier by barrier, enjoying the release, prolonging the ultimate freedom beyond.

At last the roar of the motors, muffled, sang in his head like an open song, and there was nothing between his thoughts and the world.

His mind stretched and trembled and pained from the stress, and quivered and fluttered and pulsed and throbbed and vibrated—and rejoiced.

He looked out over the wing, through the whirring propellers, at the hazy horizon, at the cloudless sky, bright and blue and infinite.

It was the best day he had ever known. It was freedom, and he had never known it before.

His mind was infinitely open as the sky above the clouds, and he stretched it out and out until he forced the limit, beyond which no mind may go, yet wanting to plunge on.

In the east, there was the dusk of night coming down, a cloak pulled up from the other side of the world by the grapple hooks of dying sunshine.

In San Francisco he phoned Hickle in Los Angeles, a man and a place so far removed that he wanted to shout to make himself heard over the telephone.

Then to a hotel—but now as a place of rest and refuge, not a symbol of flight and fear. His hate returned, beautiful, now, flower-like, delicate, to be enjoyed. To be tasted, bee-like, at his leisure.

The city outside was a whirl of lights and the lights hypnotized him with their magic. Soon he was in the streets.

There were cabs and scenes: laughter, love, death, passion—everything rolled into a capsule bundle for him. The city spread out below in a fabric of light, the hazy blue of cigar smoke closely pressing sweaty bodies, laughing mouths. A swirl of sensations.

"Somewhere else!" he cried madly to a driver.

China Town, The International Settlement, Fisherman's Wharf... The cabbies knew a tourist.

HE had been moving for hours, and now he was tired and lost, and he could not find a cab to get back to the Sir Francis Drake.

A girl and a sailor passed. A tall lithe blonde with a pert nose and high cheek bones and brown eyes heavy lips and free hips...a...blonde.

The Oholo...Lauri...was a blonde.

He began to cast up memories of her, sickeningly, making his fists clench.

He wanted a blonde to smile at him, unsuspecting. A blonde with honey colored hair and a long, slim throat with a blue vein in it, so he could watch the heart beat. He wanted to hurt the blonde, and hold her, and caress her softly, and most of all, hurt her.

He wanted to shake his fists at the sky and scream in frustration.

He wanted to find a blonde...

Finally he found one. In a small, red-fronted bar, dimly lit. She was sitting at the end of the bar, facing the door, toying with a tall drink, half-empty, from which the ice had melted.

"What'll it be, Mister?"

"Anything! Anything!" he said excitedly as he slipped behind a table, his eyes still on the woman at the bar.

"And the same for me?"

"Sure. Sure."

She brought back two drinks, picked up a bill, turned it over in her hand speculatively. She wore an off the shoulder dress, and high rouge on her Mexican cheeks. She made change from her apron, putting the money beside the second glass, sitting down in front of it, across from him.

Still he had not noticed her.

Two patrons entered. They moved to a table in the far corner near the Venetian blinds of the window and began to talk in low husky voices.

"I'll be back, dearie," the woman across from Parr said, sipping her drink, smearing the glass rim in a veined half moon.

She went to serve the girls.

When she came back Parr had brushed away the drink from in front of him.

"Listen, dearie," she said. "You got troubles?"

He grunted.

She snaked an ample hand half across the table and wiggled her shoulders to show off her breasts. "I bet I know what's wrong with you. Same as a lotta men, dearie. Want a little fun, I bet."

"Bring me that blonde," he said hoarsely.

"Listen, dearie, you don't want her. What you want…"

"The blonde!"

RELUCTANTLY she stood up, frightened by his tone. She put a hand over his change, waited.

He did not notice.

She put the money into her apron pocket, heaving her chest.

Then she got the blonde.

"You wanna buy me a drink, honey?" the blonde said.

"Sit down!"

The blonde turned to the Mexican. "Make it a double." She sat down.

"Talk!"

"Whatdaya wan' me to say, honey?"

"Just talk." He had seen the pulse in the vein in her neck. The neck was skinny, and the face was pinched, lined with heavy powder. Her eyes were weary, and her thin hands moved jerkily.

"Just talk."

When she saw his wallet, as he brought it out to pay, she said, "Maybe we oughtta go somewhere to talk." Her voice was flat and nasal, and she tossed her head. She ruffled her coarse dirty-colored hair with an automatic gesture.

Parr wanted to kill her, and his hands itched at the delicious thought.

But not tonight. Not tonight. He was too tired. He...tonight he just wanted to think about it. And then he wanted to sleep and rest and think.

She tossed off the drink. "Another one, Bess," she said shrilly, glancing at him.

He took two bills out of his wallet, two twenties, put them on the table, pushed one of them toward her without looking at it.

She drank two more shots quickly, eagerly, hungrily, as if there was need to rush through them and get them safely inside.

She leaned across the table, her eyes heavy. "I'm gonna talk, okay? Man wants to hear woman talk. Get yer kicks like that, okay. You're buyin'... Hell, I bet you think I'm a bad girl. I'm not a bed girl—bad girl." Her hands twitched drunkenly below her flat breasts. "There was a sonofabitch in my town...I came from up north, Canada." She drank again, hastily. "I could go for you, know what...I'm getting drunk, that's what. Fooled ja, didn't I? Listen. You wouldn't believe this, but I can cook. Cook. Like hell. Wouldn't think that, eh? Hell, I'm good for a lotta things. Like being walked on. Jever wanna wanna—walk on a girl? Listen. I knew a guy, once..."

Parr said, "Shut up!" For one instant, there was sickness and revulsion, and desire to comfort her, but it vanished almost before it was recognized.

She closed her mouth.

He pushed the twenty-dollar bill into her lap.

"You be here tomorrow. Tomorrow night."

"Okay."

"You be here tomorrow night."

"Sure, sure, honey."

"You be here tomorrow night, and don't forget it."

She smiled drunkenly. "I'm here…most nights, honey…"

"You be waiting for me."

"I'm always…waitin', honey. Ever since I remember, honey, waitin'. Just waitin', honey."

But the next morning, when Parr awoke, Lauri was trying to center on his open mind. She was in San Francisco, looking for him.

The depression came back, and the guilt—the knowledge of treason—that made him want to go to a mirror and stand, watching blood trickle down his face in cherry rivulets like tears.

And fear.

When he shielded, she resumed the pressure.

AT noon he was back in Los Angeles. Perspiration was under his skin, waiting icily.

He went directly to the warehouse.

Hickle, in surprise, crossed the room to him. "Mister Parr!" he said.

The right corner of Parr's mouth was twitching nervously. "Get a chair. Bring it to the desk."

When Hickle was seated before him, Parr said, "Okay. I've got some papers. I'm going to explain them to you." He got them out. "They're all alike in form. Here." He took off the top sheet and Hickle stood up to see. "This number, here, is for the truck unit." He circled it and scribbled the word "truck." "This number." He circled it. "This number is the lot number. You see, truck number nine has lots seventeen, twenty-seven, fifty-three, thirty-one."

"I get it," Hickle said.

Parr's body was trembling and he threw out a tentative wave of thought probing for the Oholo, afraid that she might come silently, knowing his approximate daytime location. He began to talk rapidly, explaining.

It was D-Day minus seven.

After fifteen minutes, he was satisfied that Hickle understood the instructions.

"There was a plain bundle this morning?"

"Yes, sir. I wondered about that."

"Get it."

Hickle got it.

Parr opened it. "Pay roll money, trucker money. Give the truckers their money when they give you their bills. I'm going to trust you, Hickle."

Hickle gulped. "Yes, sir."

Parr began to stuff money into his wallet.

She was in Los Angeles. He knew by the pressure on his mind.

"I've got to hurry. Listen. I want you to keep the workers here as long as necessary, hear? This schedule's got to be kept. And you take a thousand dollars. And listen, Hickle. This is just chicken-feed, remember that, when you're working for us."

"Yes, sir!"

He had her located, keeping his mind open to try to center on her.

HE could center on her! She was only partially shielded, and she made no protest. She was not moving, and he could...except that there was something wrong with the pressure. He was overlooking something. But she was not moving. Not yet.

"I've got to talk fast. All these final deliveries. You'll be busy. If you need help, hire it. And listen, I'll be here from time to time if I can."

"There's something wrong, Mister Parr?"

Parr searched for an excuse. "It's personal...my wife, yes, my wife, it's..." He wondered why he had used that one. It had sprung automatically to his mind. "Never mind. I'll phone in from around town. I'll try to help you all I can by phone."

She was not moving, but the pressure seemed different...*alien!*

He jerked out of his seat, kicking the chair over as he headed for the door.

A different Oholo!

There were two of them in Los Angeles!

He probed out.

Lauri was almost on top of him.

He skidded through the door, into the street, knocking a startled man out of his path.

He stared wildly in both directions. Several blocks away a cab was stalled with a red light.

And almost before him, a private car was headed uptown. With three huge leaps he was on the running board, yanking the door open.

He jerked himself in beside the frightened driver.

He twisted his head, shouting. "Emergency! Hospi..."

She had seen him trying to escape. She struck.

In the street, a flock of English sparrows suddenly faltered in flight, and one plunged blindly into the stone face of a building. The others circled hysterically, directionless, and two collided and spilled to the ground.

"Hurry, damn it!" Parr moaned at the driver. "Hurry!"

He slammed forward into the windshield, babbling.

The terrified driver stepped down on the accelerator. The car leaped forward.

Parr, fighting with all his strength, was twisted in agony, and blood trickled from his mouth.

He gasped at the driver: "Cab. Behind. Trying to kill me."

The driver was white-faced and full of movie chases and gangster headlines of shotgun killings, typical of Southern California. He had a good car under him, and he spun the wheel to the right, cutting into an alley; to the left, onto an intersecting alley; to the right, into a cross-town street; then he raced to beat a light.

He lost the cab finally in a maze of heavy traffic at Spring.

Parr was nearly unconscious, and he struggled desperately for air.

Run, run, run, he thought despairingly, because two Oholos are ten times as deadly and efficient as one…

CHAPTER EIGHT

D-DAY minus four. General mailing day.

Parr, his mind fatigued, his body tense, phoned the warehouse twice, and twice received enthusiastic reassurances behind which he could hear the hum and clatter of parcels being moved, trucks being loaded…cursing and laughing and subdued shouting.

How many hours now? His mind was clogged and stuffy and sluggish. An hour's sleep, ten minutes sleep—any time at all. If it could be spent in clear, cold, *real* sleep.

Eat, run. Always, now, he was running, afraid to stop longer than a few minutes. He needed time to *think*.

And the pressure was steady.

Get away. Leave Los Angeles!

"Parr, Parr. This is Parr," he whispered hoarsely from the back seat of the moving cab into the comset.

The rhythm of the engine, the gentle sleepy swaying of the car and the monotony of the buildings lulled him. He caught himself, shook his head savagely.

Dimly he could understand the logic advising him to remain in the city. But it was not an emotional understanding and it lacked the sharpness of reality. For now the two Oholos could follow him easily, determining his distance and direction. If he left Los Angeles, the focus of the invasion, it would be difficult to return after postal delivery. After the invasion it would be nearly impossible. It would give the Oholos added time to run him down. But to remain... His body could not stand the physical strain of four more days of continual fright, around, around, up Main—to the suburbs— to the ocean—back to Main again—down the speedway to Pasadena and through Glendale to Main. Change cabs and do it all over again.

"Yes?" the Advanceship said.

"I'm...leaving. I've got to leave. I've got to." And suddenly, in addition to the other consideration, he was afraid to be there when the invasion hit. Was it because he was afraid they knew of his treason? Or...was it because...he liked the buildings? Strangely, he did not want to see the buildings made rubble...

The answer: "You have a job to do."

"It's done!" he cried in anguish. "Everything's scheduling. In a few hours now it'll be all over. I can't do anymore here."

A pause.

"You better stay. You'll be safer there."

"I *can't!*" Parr sobbed. "They'll catch me!"

"Wait."

A honk. The purr of the engine. Clang. Bounce. Red and green lights. "…If the mailings are secure, you have the Ship's permission. Do whatever you like."

Expendable.

Parr put the comset in his coat pocket and cowered into the seat.

"Turn right!" he said suddenly to the driver. "Now…now… Right again!"

He bounced.

He closed his eyes, resting them.

"Out Hill," he said wearily without opening his eyes.

He withstood an irritated mental assault. They were tiring. But not as fast as he was.

THE silent pursuit: three cars out of the multitudes, doggedly twisting and turning through the Los Angeles streets—separated by blocks, even by miles, but bound by an unseen thread that was unbreakable.

"I gotta eat, buddy."

Parr drew himself erect. "A phone! Take me to a phone!"

The taxi ground to a stop in a service station.

Nervously, Parr began to phone airports. Three quarters of his mind was on his pursuers.

On the third try he got promise of an immediate private plane.

"Have it ready!" he ordered. Then, dropping the receiver he ran from the station to the cab.

He jockeyed for nearly thirty minutes for position.

Then he commanded the driver to abandon the intricate inter-weaving and head directly for the airport in Santa Monica.

Shortly, the two other cars swung in line, down Wilshire.

THE job of softening up Earth for the invasion began to pass entirely from the hands of the advancemen. From a ticklish, dangerous proposition at first to a virtual certain mailing day. The world wide mechanism of delivery swung into operation from time zone to time zone, and, in the scheme of conquest the advancemen passed from integral factors to inconsequential objects.

All over America, from East to West, within the space of a single day the post office became aware of the increased, the tremendously increased volume. Previously in certain sections there had been signals in the form of out-bound dribbles. Now there were in-bound floods rising suddenly to the peak intensity of overtime inundations. A million packages, some large, some small, some brown wrapped, white wrapped, light, heavy—no two alike, no way to tell the new influx from the normal handling.

At the very first each office saw the rush as a unique phenomenon for there was no reason to report it to a higher echelon which might have instituted an investigation. Merely to take care of the rush, that was all. To process the all-at-once congestion of parcels to be door to door delivered. Later to be marveled at.

Lines formed at parcel windows; trucks spewed out their cargos. Lights burned late; clerks cursed and sweated; parcels mounted higher and higher.

Nor did it break all at once in the press. The afternoon editions carried a couple of fillers about how Christmas seemed to be coming early for the citizens of Saco, Maine, and how a tiny Nevada town whose post office was cobwebby from lack of use suddenly found itself doing a land office business.

Most of the morning editions carried a whimsical AP article that the late radio newscasters picked up and rebroadcast. Then after most West Coast stations were off the air for the night events began to snowball in the East.

The breakfast newscasts carried the first stories. The morning papers began to tie in the various incidents and reach astonishing conclusions...

THE propeller was not even turning over. The plane, wheeled out of the hanger, was waiting, cold, and the pilot lounged by the office, smoking a cigarette.

The sky was black, and here and there before the blatant searchlights sprouting from dance halls and super markets, clumps of lacy California clouds fluttered like dingy sheep wool in a half-speed Mix-Master.

Parr, tossing a handful of bills at the driver, leaped from the cab and ran frantically toward the office.

The wait was terrible. Should the Oholos arrive, he was boxed in spaciously, with no escape. In gnawing at the inner side of his lower lip, he bit through his disguise into real flesh and real blood.

There were forms to sign, responsibility to be waived.

And with every minute, *they* drew nearer.

Finally the airplane motor coughed into reluctant life, and Parr could feel the coldness of artificial leather against his back.

The ship shuddered, moved heavily, shifted toward the wind onto the lighted runway. The motor roared louder and louder and the ship trembled. Slowly it began to pick up speed, the wings fighting for lift.

A searchlight from the pier made a slow ring of light toward the invisible stars.

The ground fell away and Parr was on his way to Denver.

Almost immediately, with the pressure still on his mind but fading swiftly, he fell into a fitful sleep and dreamed of treason, while, in the background ominous clouds shifted and gathered to darken the sun of his native planet. Finally, all was a starless black except for half-forgotten faces which paraded before him, telling his treason with hissing tongues in words he could not quite grasp the meaning of.

THE air of Denver was clear and bright-crystal clear, drawing in the mountains, opening up the sky like a bent back box top. The new sun seemed small.

Parr stood on a street corner acutely aware of the thin air and the bright clean sky. An open sky that seemed to be trying to talk to him. He snorted at the absurdity of the thought but he strained half consciously to listen.

He walked on, his feet tapping sharply on the concrete, his mind foggy from the uncomfortable sleep.

A building to the left momentarily reminded him of a slide shown long ago in a classroom on a distant planet, and he wondered if the picture had been taken in this city (knowing, deeply, that it could not have been).

Parr took a newspaper from a stand. Tucking it under his arm he continued to walk until he found a hotel.

He ate breakfast hurriedly in the annex and then rented a room with a radio. He went to it, lay relaxing on the bed, his mind open and free but uneasy again as he thought of treason.

"Parr," he said into the comset. "I'm in Denver."

"Have you escaped?"

"They will follow me!" Parr said wearily. "But for the moment, I'm free."

"We'll send our Denver advanceman to you," the Ship said. "The two of you should be able to handle the Oholos."

Parr's mouth was dry. He named the hotel.

"Wait, then."

He lay back but felt no exultation. He tried to force it, but there was nothing.

And then, staring at the headlines, knowledge of success broke all around him and he was trembling and jubilant. He sprang up, paced the room, moving his hands restlessly.

He rushed to the window, looked out into the street. The people below passed in a thin nervous stream. Unusually few; many more were glued at home, waiting for the mail.

A postal delivery truck turned the corner, rolled down the street before the hotel. All action ceased; all eyes turned to watch its path.

Parr wanted to hammer the wall and cry, "Stop! Stop! I've got to ask some questions first! Stop! There's something wrong!"

PARR was shaking. He sat on the bed and began to laugh. But his laughter was hollow.

His victory—a Knoug victory... He frowned. Why had he automatically made a differentiation where there should be none? He realized that the mailing success had released him from nervous preoccupation in Knoug work; for the first time he was free of responsibility, and he could think...clearly...about... He wanted to hammer the terrifying new *doubts* out of his mind. But they gathered like rain clouds. He went to the mirror and fingered his face. "What's wrong? What's wrong?" Knoug victory had a bitter taste.

He suddenly pictured the civilization around him as a vast web held in tension by a vulnerable thread of co-operation, now slowly disintegrating as the thread crumbled. And he took no joy in the thought.

He began to let images float in his mind. Imagined scenes, taking place beyond the walls.

A man went in to payoff a loan, his pockets stuffed with money.

"I'm not taking it."

"What sa matter? It's legal tender. You *gotta* take it."

Bills on the counter.

"You didn't earn that!"

"It don't matter."

"It isn't any good. Everybody's got it."

"That don't *matter.*"

"It's worthless!"

"Yeah? Listen: 'For all debts, public and private…'"

Parr's mind reached out to grasp the unsettling immensity of it. He flipped on the radio, half heard an excited announcer.

Parr thought: All over the world, each to his own: coins, bills, dollars, rupees, pesos, pounds—how many million parcels were there? Each stuffed with enough to make its owner a man of wealth, as wealth was once measured.

Parr thought it was terrifying, somehow.

And the headline of the paper admitted: "No Test To Reveal Good Money From Bad."

(There was a mob. They were storming a liquor store, while the owner cowered inside. He was waiting for the police. But the police were too busy elsewhere, so finally, to salvage what he could before the mob took his stock for nothing he opened the door, crying, "Form a line! Form a line!")

Parr thought of the confusion that would grow.

Prices spiraling.

(In the United States Senate, a member took the floor to filibuster until California had its mail delivery and its fair share of the free money.)

This was the day work stoppages would begin.

FAMINE PREDICTED…PRESIDENT IN APPEAL TO…GUARD MOBILIZED…

Riots. Celebrations. (A church burned the mortgage gratefully.) Clean shelves. Looming scarcity.

By the time the sun dipped into the Pacific, the whole economic structure of the world would be in shambles.

Governments doubtless would blame each other (half-heartedly), propose new currency, taxes, and the gold standard again.

Industrial gears would come unmeshed as workers took vacations. Electric power, in consequence would begin to fail.

(Looting already occupied the attention of the better part of the underworld, and not a few respectable citizens decided to get it now and store it for use when it would be unavailable because others had done likewise.)

Stagnation tomorrow. But as yet, the fear and hysteria had not really begun. Parr shuddered, sickened. "What have I *done?*"

It would take months to unmuddle the chaos.

Earth was ripe for invasion...

PARR aroused from a heavy stupor. The pressure was back. He moaned, and the knock on the door jolted him into startled animal movement.

The knob turned. Parr tensed, although he could tell that the Oholo team was still distant. "Who is it?"

The door opened and a disguised Knoug slipped through. Immediately behind him a simian-like Earthman towered. "Come in," the Knoug said. When they were inside, he shut the door.

"The Ship sent me over," the Knoug said. "You wanted help? My name's Kal. You probably remember me on Ianto?"

Parr swung his legs from the bed and stood up. "You feel the pressure?"

Kal rumbled angrily.

"Two Oholos," Parr said. "I've been dodging them."

"Two, eh? Okay. It's a good thing I brought Bertie along. Two, you say. Well I'll be damned."

Kal turned to the Earthman. "There'll be two, Bertie. So watch yourself…"

Bertie grunted noncommittally.

"Okay. Now like I told you, shoot when I give you the mental signal. You'll see the ones."

"Uh-huh," Bertie said, chewing complacently.

"Go on downstairs then."

Bertie hunkered forward and leered at Parr. "Sure. Sure."

"Hurry the hell up," Kal said.

Bertie shuffled to the door, opened it, left the room.

Parr swallowed uneasily.

Kal chuckled. "Good one, Bertie. Useful. Damn this pressure. Glad I brought him. They won't be looking for an Earthman, eh? So when they try to come in here after us, he'll drop 'em, eh?"

Parr wet his lips. "They're getting nearer."

"Relax," Kal said. He crossed to the bed and sat down. "The Fleet's out. It just came out. Did you hear?"

PARR felt a shock of surprise. He imagined the hundred powerful ships of the fleet coming, one by one, from the dead isolation of hyperspace. In his mind's eye he could see the faint glimmer of the static shield—the protective aura— form slowly in real space; he could imagine the ships safe within their electric sheaths which caught the hull-wrenching force of transition and dissipated it from the heavy steel plating. He could imagine one ship—perhaps one—popping out, shieldless, battered by the force vortex, and perhaps leaking air or ruptured entirely because the protective aura had collapsed under pressure. Then he saw the ships neatly pulling into formation, grouping for instructions, waiting for the attack signal.

"Day after tomorrow they attack," Kal said.

"They're closer," Parr whispered.

Kal concentrated. "Yeah. I feel them. Come to the window." He stood up and crossed the room in quick cat-like strides.

Parr followed him and the two of them stared down. Perspiration stood on Parr's forehead. After a moment they saw Bertie come out from beneath the hotel awning. He seemed small at a distance, and they saw him toss a cigarette butt carelessly to the sidewalk. He moved leisurely away from the entrance and leaned against the side of the hotel, one hand in his overcoat pocket.

Kal sneered, "You think they'll drive right up?"

Parr's face twitched. "I don't know…if they know there's two of us…" He glanced left along the street. "I guess they will. I guess they'll try to come right in after us."

Kal chuckled. "That's good. That's damned good, eh?"

Parr turned to stare at him. "They're strong."

"They won't be looking for Bertie."

"Listen," Parr whispered hoarsely. "They're stronger than we are."

Kal snarled a curse.

"No," Parr said intently. "They are."

"Shut up!"

"Listen," Parr said. "I know. I've…"

Kal turned slowly. "They're not stronger. They *couldn't* be stronger. Even if Bertie misses, we'll get them. If they're so strong, why haven't they already carried the fight to us? If they're so strong, they should be ready to attack us, so why don't they?"

He turned back to the window.

"They're almost here," Parr said.

A cab turned the corner. "Feel them center on us?" Parr said, drawing down his shield as tightly as he could.

Kal, tense-faced, nodded.

Parr stared fascinated as the cab screeched to a halt.

Then Parr felt a wave of sickness and uncertainty; he reached out for Kal's elbow. "Wait!" he cried.

But already, below, Bertie jerked into explosive action.

He shot three times. The male Oholo pitched forward to the gutter.

Bertie's gun exploded once more, but the muzzle was aimed into the air. He crumpled slowly, and the gun clinked to the sidewalk from nerveless fingers.

"He got one," Kal said in satisfaction. "The other one must be quicker 'n hell."

Parr let out a tired sigh.

"That's that," Kal said. "...I'll be damned, a female Oholo! She won't dare to try two of us alone."

Parr's eyes were fixed below. In what seemed a dream, he watched her get out of the cab. She glanced up and down the street. She looked up, quickly, toward their window. And then she darted across the sidewalk toward the hotel entrance.

"I'll be damned!" Kal cried. "She's coming up anyway!" His eyes sparkled gleefully. He searched his lips with his tongue. "Let's both hit her now! She's near enough!"

"No!" Parr cried sharply. "No! Let her get closer... Let's...let's make sure we get her."

They could feel her nearing them, not quickly, not slowly, but with measured steps.

CHAPTER NINE

SHE was just outside the door and Parr felt something like momentary confusion before the hate came. Yet when it did it was tinged and colored as he thought of her walking toward them, alone. He tried to concentrate on her remembered image, tried to call up the previous hate in all its glory. He could not; instead, even the hate he knew drained away. In its place he felt—not fear exactly—not fear for himself but of the inevitability of death. Not his death—hers.

He saw Kal's lips curl, and then he winced. Fingernails dug into his palms.

And the door opened and she stood before them. There was a breathless instant, absolutely still, while time hung fire. Her eyes were aflame. Eyes, he knew, that were capable of softness as well. Eyes steady, intent, unafraid. He was frozen in delicious surprise that tingled his spine, and he felt his scalp crawl. He also felt deep awe at her courage.

She came into the room, closed the door, stood with her back leaning lightly against it. Her eyes blazed into his.

Her red lips moved delicately. "Hello," she said. "I've been looking for you." She had not glanced at Kal.

"Now!" Kal cried wildly.

Parr wanted to scream something meaningless, but before the sound could bubble forth the room seemed to erupt into a colored blaze. She had struck at him with a lethal assault!

He reeled, fighting back for his life, conscious now of Kal fighting at his side.

Her eyes were steady, and her face frowned in concentration. She was icy calm in the struggle and there was cold fury in her whips of thought. But slowly, under their resistance, her eyes began to widen in surprise.

For a breath-held moment, even with the two of them against her, the issue seemed in doubt; Kal half crumpled, stunned by a blast of hot thought that seared away his memory for one instant.

She could not turn fast enough to Parr, nor could she, in feinting his automatic attack, strike again at Kal. Then again, the two of them were together, and slowly, very slowly, they hedged her mind between them and shielded it off.

Kal recovered.

Parr gritted his teeth in a mental agony he could not account for and stripped at her outer shield. Kal came in too and the shield began to break.

The Oholo still stood straight and contemptuous in defeat, her eyes calm and deadly as she still struggled against them.

She struck once more with fading strength and Parr caught the thrust and shunted it away. And then he was in her mind.

HE held a stroke that would burn like a sun's core, and almost hurled it. But there was a great calmness before him and he hesitated a fraction of a second in doubt as he stared deep into her glazing eyes. He felt his heart throb in new pain.

Kal struck over him, and the Oholo went limp, suddenly, and sank unconscious to the floor, a pathetic rag doll. A tiny wisp of thought struggled out and faded.

Kal cried in triumph and gathered for the final blow.

Great, helpless rage tore at Parr then, and almost before he realized it he sent a powerful blast into Kal's relaxing shield. Kal rocked to his heels, dazed, and his left hand went to his eyes. He whirled, lax mouthed, surprised.

"What...?"

"She's mine!" Parr screamed wildly, "She's mine!"

"The hell—"

In fury Parr slapped the other Knoug a stinging blow across the mouth. "Get out! Get out! Get out or I'll kill you!"

Kal's eyes glazed in surprise.

Parr was panting. "I'll finish her," he gasped. "Now get out!"

Kal's eyes met his for a moment but they could not face the anger in Parr's.

"Get out or I'll kill you!" Parr said levelly, his mind a welter of emotions that he could not sort out and recognize.

Kal rubbed his cheek slowly. "Okay," he said hoarsely. "Okay."

Parr let breath out through his teeth. "Hurry!"

Kal's lips curled. His shoulders hunched and he seemed about to charge. But Parr relaxed, for he saw fear in the Knoug's eyes. Kal straightened. He shrugged his shoulders indifferently, spat on the carpet without looking at Parr and stepped over the unconscious Oholo. He jerked the door open and without looking back slammed it behind him.

Parr was trembling and suddenly emotionally exhausted.

PARR'S knees were water. He stared fascinated at the fallen Oholo. He sank to the bed. He let his thoughts touch her unconscious mind as it lay exposed and helpless, and he wondered why he did not strike the death blow. He tried to think of stripping her mind away slowly, layer by layer, until she lay a helpless babbling infant, her body weak and pliant to his revenge. But he thought of her clear eyes and he was sickened and ashamed.

He called up memories of Oholos—the captured few— and now for the first time he knew general respect rather than hate. And thinking of Knougs, he writhed.

Yet he was conditioned to hate and he was conditioned to kill. He must kill, for the conditioning was strong. He tried to fight down the revolt of his thoughts, and, in recognizing the revolt at last, knowledge came. The guilt of treason. Not for any act. His treason was doubt, and doubt was weakness, and weakness was death. He could not be weak for the weak are destroyed. But he seemed, for a heartbeat, to see through the fabric of Empire, which was not strength at all. No he thought, I've believed too long. It's in my blood. There's nothing else.

He went to the wash basin and drew a glass of water. He carried it to the Oholo, knelt by her head and bathed her temple with his dampened handkerchief until she moaned and threw an arm weakly over her forehead. Her hand met his, squeezed, relaxed, and was limp again.

He carried her to the bed and sat beside her, staring at her clear face, which was an Earthface. (I've been in this body too long, he thought, I'm beginning to think all wrong.) For the face was not without beauty for him.

He shook his head dazedly, trying to understand himself.

(Here is the enemy, he thought. How do I know? I have been told ever since I can remember. But is it true? Does saying it make it true? But what else can I believe? One must believe something!)

SHE opened her eyes, stared at him uncomprehending. He waited patiently as she gathered her loose thoughts and tied them down. She smiled uncertainly, not yet recognizing him.

Finally he could see understanding in her eyes.

"Your mind is too weak to fight," he said. "If you try to shield I will kill you."

Her lips curled. "What do you want?"

"Don't try to shield," he warned. He studied her face and his chest was tight. He looked away from her face.

"I've got to ask you some questions," he said. "After that, I'm going to kill you."

There was no fear in Lauri's eyes. "Go ahead," she said calmly. "Kill me."

"I...I...want to ask you something first," he said. "I've got to ask you some questions."

Her lips glistened and he felt sympathy that he could not understand. And seeing her frown, he shielded the thoughts from her.

"You're not…quite like I thought you were," she said, very calmly.

"I am!" he snarled. "I am what you thought!" He was ashamed of the sympathy he had let her sense, and then he was ashamed of being ashamed, and his mind was confusion.

"Why did you—did you leave this planet as an unprotected flank, like this?" he said. It was a question, he knew, that had to be answered, before…before…what?

"They weren't ready to join us," she said.

"What do you mean?"

"They were not developed enough to join us," she said.

"Why didn't you conquer them!" he insisted. "You were strong enough. Why didn't you conquer them?"

She said: "We couldn't do that. We don't have any right to do that."

In that instant, it all became clear. Suddenly truth overwhelmed him, wave after wave, like a sickness. "No!" he cried. "No!" He dropped his head into his hands. "Lies," he murmured. "Lies, lies, lies!" He saw the wrongness, the terrible wrongness, and he searched desperately over his life for repudiation, an excuse. But he found none.

They had come to him and said, This is the law of life. And they took him and trained him, and showed him nothing else. He had been scarcely a child at the first school of soldiery, and they had fashioned his mind, a pliant mind, and ground doubts out (if there had been any.) They told him that the law was strength, and strength was destiny, and destiny was to rule those below, obey those above, and destroy those who did not agree. There were no friends and enemies—only the rulers and the ruled. And the ruler must expand or die of admitted weakness.

"It's all lies!" he said. He felt the crumbling away of the certainty he had lived by. And before the helpless Oholo he felt weak and defeated and suddenly he realized that his mind shield was down.

She reached out gently to touch him.

Below, a police siren wailed in the streets. A car for corpses.

HE tried to shake the hand away. "They lied," he said. "They lied about everything. They lied that you were ready to conquer us. They told us you were cowardly and would kill us if we did not kill you first, and that we must take…"

She said: "It was worse than we thought. We did not think you were strong enough to attack us. Not here. We thought if we let you alone you would collapse of your own weight."

"I never knew," he said. "There wasn't any way to know. You have to do what everyone else does. You get to think they must be right." He made a small sound. "When I first came here—it started to bother me, when I saw the planet was unprotected—when I saw how strong you were… But I had so many things to do. I was too busy to think. But I felt something at the very first about your presence here…"

She stirred restlessly on the bed. He knew that he was defenseless before her because she had recovered, but she did not strike out. "Trying to help them," she said. "A few of us came to help them. They needed us. We were trying to prevent a war. And a few more years—if we'd…but that's gone now. You'll destroy it all."

He stood from the bed and it creaked.

"We were slowly changing their governments," she said. "We would have succeeded." He felt her mind slowly gather, and there was infinite bitterness, and he tensed. But still she did not strike at him.

"I want you to go," Parr said. "Before the other Knoug comes back. Get out."

Words damned up inside him. He had been trained to hate and trained to kill. The emotions were loose now. There was no outlet for them. He was frustrated and enraged. Hate bubbled about in him, fermenting. He had been trained to hate and to kill. Lauri winced as she felt the turmoil. "Get out!" he screamed.

The door crashed open.

Three figures lunged through.

"Lauri, thank God!" one of them cried. "We thought he'd killed you."

Parr suddenly found his arms held by two Oholos.

"We got here as soon as we could pick up your thoughts."

Lauri said, "Jen is already dead."

One of the Oholos slapped Parr's face savagely. "We'll kill this one for that!" he snarled.

LAURI sprang from the bed and sent the weapon spinning from the hand of the leader of the three Oholos. He gave a startled gasp. The weapon hit the carpet and slammed to rest against the far wall. "Don't!" she cried.

"You're crazy!" the leader snarled. "What's wrong with you?"

"He saved my life," Lauri said, panting.

"He's Knoug," the leader sneered.

"You know damned well he was trying to use you for something or other."

Parr stared, fascinated. He was surprised to find that he was not afraid. The shock of capture had not yet passed, and he seemed to be watching a drama from which he was removed.

"No!" Lauri said. "No, he wasn't!"

"How can you say that, Lauri? Look what he's done! Look what he's already done!"

"Unshield, Parr, show them," Lauri commanded.

Parr hesitated, trying to divine the plot and see what was required of him.

"It's a trick," the leader said. "They've got some way to fool us, even with an open mind!"

Lauri's eyes were wide.

The leader jerked his hand. "Kill him," he instructed.

The Oholo on Parr's left released Parr's arm and reached inside his coat for a weapon.

Lauri darted across the room and pounced on the weapon lying at the base of the wall. She seized it and rolled over. She aimed it steadily at the Oholo on Parr's left. "Don't do that," she said. "Let him go." She got to one knee.

PARR felt the grip ease on his right arm. He stood free. And for the first time—with strange hope—the feeling of unreality vanished.

"You're insane!" the Oholo on Parr's right rasped.

She jerked the muzzle of the weapon. "I told you. He saved my life. He could have killed me. He didn't."

"A trick!"

"Get away from him!"

Reluctantly the two stood back, and the leader shifted uneasily on his feet.

"Don't you try it," Lauri suggested. "For all you know, I might really shoot. You aren't that quick."

Parr let out his breath.

"You!" she snapped at him. "Get to the door!"

Dazed, he obeyed her. He shook his head to clear it. He was afraid they would try to stop him.

"Open it!"

He opened the door and hesitated, looking at her.

"I'm coming," she snapped. Still covering the three Oholos she got to her feet and began to back toward him. "Don't follow," she warned the three before her.

"You know what this means?" the leader said. "You know what it means to help the enemy?"

"Go on out," she told Parr. "He saved my life," she said doggedly.

He obeyed. She followed him. She fumbled for the doorknob, found it. "Run!" she cried. She slammed the door.

They ran desperately for the stairs. Their feet pounded on the soft carpet as they clattered down.

She was almost abreast of him. "Help me!" she cried when they passed the first landing. And a moment later Parr knew what she meant. They were trying to tear into his mind, and she was holding them off with her own shield. He joined her as well as he could, marveling at the vast strength she had recovered.

"Hurry!" she cried. "I can't hold it much longer." She lurched into him and he put an arm around her waist.

AND then they were through the lobby and into the silent street. No curious spectators were lingering to stare at the drying patch of dirty brown in the gutter beyond the awning.

"This way!" she cried.

As they fled on the pressure weakened. She was running fleetly at his side now, her brow unfurrowed, and yet he knew that she was still holding the shield under terrific pressure.

"In here," she gasped, suddenly turning into a narrow alleyway. "Stop!" she said. She half dragged him down to the pavement behind a row of packing crates.

"They'll be right after us!" he panted.

"No. Listen. Follow my lead. I think I can blanket us, if you help me."

Parr felt the warmth of her thoughts around him, and then they began to go up beyond his range and he had to strain to stay with them. Underneath her thoughts his mind began to quiet, and, in a moment he felt—isolation.

"Help, here," she said.

He saw the weakness and strengthened it. With her help, he found the range less high, and he could relax under it. And their minds were very close together, and their thoughts were completely alone. "We're safe here," she whispered.

He listened to his own far away breathing, and heard hers, too, softer but labored.

They crouched, waiting, and the street before them was quiet in the sunlight, for the mail trucks were out, and no taxis moved. The city—for the moment—was deathly still and waiting uneasily. The high air was sharp in his lungs.

"They've missed us," she said at length. "Wait! They're... They're after...it's another Knoug. They think we've separated, and they think it's you."

"That would be Kal," Parr said. "He must have been waiting nearby." He brought out the comset. "He must have seen us come out together."

He flicked open the comset, heard, "...joined with the Oholos. Parr and the other just left the hotel together."

"He's told the Advanceship," Parr said to the girl.

"It doesn't make any difference," Lauri replied wearily.

And Parr breathed a nervous sigh, for the hate had found its channel. The Empire had made him unclean and debased him, and he had to cleanse himself. His vast reserve of hate shrieked out against the Empire; their own weapon turned against them.

"I'd like to get back to the Advanceship," Parr said. "If I could get back, I could smash in their faces!"

"Oh," she said.

THE comset sputtered excitedly. "Three Oholos after me! They're armed! Must be new ones. The other two weren't armed!"

The comset was silent.

"Three?" Parr said. "That's right, there were three. I thought there were just five on the whole planet."

"There's about fifty now. They landed last night. Out in the Arizona desert. They're the only ones who could get here in time."

Parr felt elation. But it passed.

"Fifty... That's not enough to stop the invasion."

"It's all we could get here," Lauri repeated.

Parr groaned. "The Knougs will shield the planet tomorrow. It will trap those fifty on the surface. And us. They'll shoot us, if we're lucky. But I'd like to kill some first!"

The comset crackled, and the Ship voice said: "How many new ones altogether?"

"I don't know," Kal answered. "I only know of three."

"We'll hurry the attack, then, before they're set. Can you hold out, Kal?"

"I don't know," Kal said.

The attack. The meaning of it suddenly rang in Parr's ears. Until a second ago, he had seen his hate as personal, and now he realized that the Empire was ready to capture a planet and then to destroy a System. And he saw the vast evil of the Empire hurtling toward Oholo civilization. He gnashed his teeth.

Lauri's hand jerked on Parr's elbow. "The one you call Kal is dead."

"I'm glad," Parr was grim. He remembered the savage eyes, which the Earth disguise could not conceal. "I'm glad."

"Kal, Kal," the Advanceship called into emptiness. "Kal! Come in, advanceman Kal!"

Parr flipped off the comset.

She lowered the thought blanket completely. "Relax. Try to relax."

"Why did you do it?" he said. "Why didn't you let them kill me?"

"I don't know," she said slowly. "You saved my life. I couldn't let them kill you. I saw how you felt, how you suddenly changed. How you'd become a new person all at once. I couldn't pass judgment on you after that. I hated you and then I didn't hate you anymore. It doesn't matter. It's too late to matter. I...I..."

Her mind was warm against his. "They're going back to join the others in the desert now," she said. "They're going to get ready to fight the attack."

"Lauri," Parr said. "Lauri, I've got to do something!"

CHAPTER TEN

(New York had broken windows now, and the streets were glass littered. An occasional white face peered out suspiciously from above a ground floor. But the heartbeat of subways was stilled. The cry had been: "You'll *starve* in the City!" and there had been an hysterical exodus, slow at first and then faster and faster and faster. The moon marched her train of shadows in the cavern streets.)

In Denver, the moon rode the mountains, calm, misted, serene.

"Parr," he spoke into the comset, and he felt Lauri's hand tighten on his elbow.

He glanced nervously at the sky. He was afraid to see the planet shield blossom as it might any minute to signify the attack had begun. But he feared even worse the absence of it.

"Parr?" the Advanceship spat back.

"The Oholos have a defense system around their own planets. *It won't do you any good to capture this one! You won't be able to get nearer!*"

"You are guilty of treason, Parr!"

"You can't get at their inner system! They have a defense ring that can blast your Fleet out of space."

"Lies!"

Parr glanced at Lauri beside him in the darkness. "No!" he said. "They are stronger than you are!"

"They would have attacked us if they were," the Knoug said calmly.

"They don't think like that!"

"A poor bluff, Parr."

"Stop!" Parr said, "Listen…" He looked at Lauri again. "No use. They cut off."

"I didn't think they'd bluff," Lauri said. She looked across the street. The street lights had come on on schedule, but they soon flickered out as the power supply waned. The city was dark.

"Will they scorch the planet?"

PARR glanced once more at the sky. "I think they're holding off trying to gain new information on your Oholos. Or maybe they're having trouble getting ready. We'll know very soon whether they'll scorch it or assault it with an occupation force."

Lauri said, "You tried."

"If we could *convince* them, like I was convinced…if we could show them you *were* strong and peaceful…"

"But we aren't strong, Parr. They caught us unprepared. If we had a year or two…"

"How long would it be before you could get reinforcements here?"

Lauri bit her lower lip. "At least a month. We'd have to organize the units and everything. No sooner."

"Oh."

"What were you thinking?"

"I thought," Parr said. "...I thought I might hold the attack off...for as much as a couple of hours."

"That wouldn't help."

Parr swallowed and cleared his throat nervously. "I don't know. Maybe it would give the Oholos more time to prepare. It might help a little."

"How?"

"I'm going to try that. I've got to do something, Lauri."

He flipped open the comset and started to speak, but the channel was already busy. It was filled with crackling explosive Knoug language.

Parr began to listen intently.

It was a conversation between the Flagship and one of the other ships of the Fleet. "...Parr's right," the other ship said. "So they're down there. They say they've fought Oholos, and he's probably right..."

"How many are there?" the Flagship demanded.

"Thirteen. All in the engine room."

"Tell them Parr was bluffing," the Flagship ordered.

"I already did."

"Tell them they're guilty of mutiny!"

"I did, and they still won't come out. They're the bunch that were in the assault at Coly. They've been hard to handle ever since."

"All right. Go after them with guns..."

"What is it?" Lauri asked.

"Shhhh!" Parr cautioned.

A third circuit opened. "No other ship reports trouble. It's just this one bunch."

THERE was a harsh curse, guttural and nasty. "These channels are open! The whole Fleet knows about that Coly bunch now!"

"What in hell! *Damn it, get them off!* We've got to isolate…" Click.

Parr stared at the comset in his hand.

Parr smiled thinly. "I did a little good, at least. A bunch of veterans must have been listening in on me… One of the Fleet ships has a little trouble."

"Maybe…" she began excitedly.

"No," Parr said. "It was only thirteen Knougs. It's scarcely a ripple. It might make the rest of the Fleet a little uneasy—but they'll still take orders. I'm sorry Lauri, but it's not going to help much."

"How do you know it won't?" she insisted.

The bitter smile was still there. "I've seen something like it before. In five minutes it will all be over."

"Oh."

"Well," he said after a moment, "I better try to get the Ship. I'm going to hold them off as long as I can."

He clicked open the comset again.

"Kal," he lied icily. "Advanceman Kal." For the first time he was glad of the tinny, voice-disguising diaphragm.

"Get off!" the Advanceship ordered. "This is the Commander. We're under communication security, damn it!"

PARR nodded to himself in recognition of what had happened. Commanders were now on the whole communications network. It would prevent ordinary operators from spreading more news of mutiny through the Fleet; it would blanket the manufacturing of rumors. And, if things were running true to course the Flagship was monitoring all channels just in case.

"I've found out the Oholo's disposition," Parr hissed into the tiny comset. "Can you pick me up?"

There was a momentary pause.

"…We thought you were dead, Kal. Why didn't you answer our calls?"

"…Broke my comset," Parr lied quickly. "I've just killed the traitor, Parr, and I'm using his."

There seemed to be suspended judgment in the Ship.

"If you pick me up, I can give you details. But you'll have to hurry! Two Oholos are closing in right now!"

"How many are there altogether?"

Parr hesitated. "Only twenty, Parr said. I think less than that. It won't be necessary to scorch the planet."

Again silence. Then the Flagship itself cut in, "All right. We'll pick you up. Where are you?"

"Denver." He made out the street signs in the darkness. "I'm here at a street corner. Eighteenth and Larimer."

"Someone who knows the territory from the Advanceship can pick you up. Ten minutes. Hold on."

"Hurry!" Parr pleaded.

He cut off the comset. He realized he was frightened. The night was growing cold and he took two deep breaths. He let the comset slip from his fingers and shatter on the pavement. He kicked it away in savage annoyance, and snarled a curse.

Lauri shuddered inwardly at his violence, but he did not notice. And she forced a smile and touched him with a warm thought.

"I told them I was Kal," he said. "I…asked them to pick me up."

Lauri half gasped in surprise.

"They'll hold off the attack until they hear from me again. I'll try to keep them guessing as long as I can."

He was tired. He and Lauri had been walking the streets aimlessly for hours. At first there had been mobs after the mail delivery. Then the governor, conscious of what had happened in some Eastern cities, had declared martial law and only soldiers were supposed to be on the streets after sundown curfew. Already many people had fled the city in terror.

AS he and Lauri walked side by side, Parr felt he had come to know her better than he had ever known anyone. He realized how strong his mind had grown under its month long test, and he knew that she had come to respect his strength, she who was so strong herself. But it was not her strength he respected. Strangely, it was her weakness—her compassion and her ability to forgive. An unknown thing, forgiveness, a beautiful thing.

She stood silently beside him. Then she said, "What time you gain won't matter."

"Maybe it will!" he said harshly, hating the Empire.

She stared into his face. She shook her head. "No," she said. She touched his cheek. "I ought to say something."

"What do you mean?"

"I don't know. That it's a brave thing you want to do…"

"After what I've done, I've got to do something to make up for my life."

"What you did doesn't matter anymore."

"Listen," he said. "Listen, Lauri. You better leave. Don't stand here any longer."

She did not move.

He gritted his teeth. "Hurry up!"

Her mind touched his gently, cloud-like, and drew away. "Let me go with you."

"You know that wouldn't work." After a minute she turned reluctantly.

"Wait!" he cried after she had gone only a few steps.

Eagerly she turned.

"Listen!" He glanced at his watch. "Listen. The Fleet is nervous. The Knougs are nervous. It might not take much after that Coly bunch revolted… They're yellow inside, and the seeds of doubt are there. If we could just make them believe you really had a weapon. An hour from now—give me *one hour*—you're to contact the Fleet on my comset and tell them the Oholos are going to destroy their Advanceship right before their eyes. Then tell them to get out, the whole Fleet, or you'll destroy every ship. That may make them think! That may make them believe!"

"But unless the Ship really is destroyed before their eyes..."

"I'll take it into hyperspace without a shield. One minute it will be there, the next minute it won't. Maybe they won't stop to figure it out."

"But you'll be killed!"

"GIVE me just one hour. Go on, damn it. Don't argue!" She seemed ready to cry. Then she bit her lip.

"But—Parr! Parr! I *can't!* How can I? *You broke the comset!*"

Parr's mind was dazed. He tried to think. "...Listen. Find the one Kal had! See if you can find that! You've got to, Lauri. It all depends on that. You've just *got to* find it!"

She hesitated.

"Don't argue," he insisted. "Hurry! They'll be after me any minute."

She seemed to want to say something.

"Run!" he cried. And then she was hurrying away and her mind left his entirely, so there would be no danger of detection when the scout ship came for him. And then she turned a corner, and was gone...

THE silver saucer shaped scout ship zipped down the street, banked sharply and vanished, recording (Parr knew) electronic details for its mothership, the pick-up craft.

Parr waited, his mouth dry.

Finally—after what seemed a long time—he saw the dark, moving patch return. It lowered, and Parr could make out the details of the unlighted surface. He sighed with relief. Fortunately it was the small three passenger craft.

It hovered, closed on the intersection and settled. Hoping that neither of its crew knew him by sight, Parr sprinted from the shadows of the building to the opening door.

The distance seemed to unravel before his feet, lengthening like a magic carpet.

His feet hit the edge of the door almost together and grasping the sides he pulled himself in, falling forward and gasping for the crew's benefit, "Oholos!"

The inside of the craft, operating under low flying procedure, was darkened except for the dull orange of the instruments.

"Up!" Parr cried in Knoug, and the craft shot away pressing him to the floor even though the acceleration compensator was whirring in his ears.

He groaned and stiffened, anticipating the light when they were in second procedure level.

He heard one of the crew say: "Pick-up successful."

"Can you berth your craft on the Flagship?"

PARR felt a dread for he had thought to go to the Advanceship, and that was the one Lauri would name for destruction!

Relief came when the crewman said, "Wrong hanger sort. This isn't combat equipment, sorry."

"All right."

Parr breathed an easier sigh, and the communications set went off.

The lights came on.

Instinctively Parr lowered his head into his arms. He groaned again. "My leg," he mumbled.

"What?"

"Hurt my leg," he lied.

A crewman knelt beside him. Parr realized then that they were carrying an extra crewman.

The Knoug rolled him over. There was a startled gasp of recognition and Parr hit him in the neck. He slumped down and Parr had to squirm from under his limp body.

"What the—!"

Parr was on his feet.

"That's not Kal!" one of the others said.

The pilot swiveled around.

Parr dove, realizing, even as he was in the air that each Knoug was reaching for his focus gun.

He hit the standing Knoug. The Knoug teetered. Parr hit him again.

The pilot had his gun out.

Parr slammed a mental bolt at the pilot and he was surprised to see that the shield folded like hot butter. Even had he wished to he could not have stopped his assault from crisping the other's thoughts to oblivion. He was almost annoyed at the weakness.

He tried a mental assault at the other sagging crewman with equal results.

The craft started to spin out of control.

Parr struggled forward, was slammed sideways, and far below he could see moonlight flash on water.

He was thrown into the controls on the second spin, and he pulled back the emergency equalizer in desperation. The craft skittered.

And then he was in control.

He found the beam on the dial. He was to the left. He centered on it and followed it in.

He jockeyed below the gaping hatch of the Advanceship and came up slowly. The controls were stiff. It was a ticklish job.

Then he was inside. He shied left to set the craft down.

It bounced and half-rolled on the deck. Then he struggled to the door.

When he opened it there was an orderly waiting. "That was a hell of a landing," he said. "For—hey!"

He went down easily under the assault. Parr realized his mind had grown even stronger than he had supposed. For the first time he began to hope that he really stood a chance of making it.

He glanced at his watch.

Almost forty-five minutes! It had seemed only five...

LAURI ran toward the second building. Her mind usually smooth and calm, was now a welter of conflicting thoughts. She had tried to reach the other Oholos. But they shut themselves off. No help from them.

There were no cabs out. And the telephones were dead. She was desperately afraid Kal was in the morgue but she could not risk the time to be sure. Vaguely she remembered the siren that had squalled when the police came for the body of the Oholo and his Earth assailant who had been killed outside the hotel. But she could not remember another siren near the time Kal had been killed. She was forced to assume the police had not come for him.

But she could not be sure.

If the police had not come, she reasoned, then he had not been killed before witnesses. Therefore he had not been killed in the streets.

She knew that he had seen them leave the hotel. That narrowed the range. That he had been killed shortly afterward by the Oholos narrowed the range even more.

He had not been moving when he was killed, and he had just finished reporting Parr's and her flight, meaning that he had been stationary since his observation. And there would be no reason for the Oholos to move or to hide the body.

Therefore his body should be where it had fallen.

There had been four business buildings in the vicinity where a man could have been killed unseen.

She pushed open the doors to the second. The ground floor, within observation range, was easily checked. So was the second. Third. Fourth. Fifth.

She was back in the street. Two more buildings. Half her time gone. She glanced at her watch for verification. Each of the two remaining buildings had four floors.

The nearest one was locked. But there was a light inside. She was puzzled. Then she saw the cleaning maid come down the front stairs, carrying a brace of candles in one hand and a mop and bucket in the other. The old woman moved slowly, unconcerned, oblivious of the outside world, intent only on her job. Lauri shuddered, but she knew that the face would not be calm if she had seen a corpse in her duties. Therefore, there was no corpse inside.

One building left!

But a few minutes later she was back in the streets. There had been nothing on the lower floor, the second floor, and the two top floors needed only a glance.

She sobbed desperately.

Something had been wrong with her reasoning, and she had only twenty minutes left to start from the beginning and find the Knoug's body.

PARR ran quickly along the corridor. He passed two incurious Knougs. He continued on, winding upward toward the control room which he had to capture. There would be a delicate balance of timing and luck between success and failure.

He was not frightened now, even though he knew he could not personally win the fight in capture or success. His mind was calm. Strangely, too, it was at peace.

He clambered up the final ladder, his hands unsteady on the rungs. The control room door was closed. He tensed, listening, wondering how many of the enemy were inside.

He knocked, his knuckles brittle on steel. He thought, in that fleet second, of Lauri. He wondered dimly if she had found the comset.

"Yeah?"

"I've got Kal out here, sir!" Parr said briskly, hoping to imitate the orderly's voice.

"What the hell!" a voice from inside roared, "I thought we told you to take him down to the Commander's office."

Parr held his breath.

He heard an indistinct mutter of voices inside and he knew that one of them must be on the inter-phone to the Commander.

"Something screwy here!" the voice roared indignantly.

Parr hit the door and it crashed inward with an echoing clang.

He catapulted into the congested control room. In a glance he saw there were only two Knougs. One was at the control banks, half turned in surprise. The other held the phone limply in his left hand, his eyes staring.

Parr kicked the door shut viciously and the sound rang in his ears. He launched himself at the Knoug with the phone. He felt his head meet a soft stomach and he heard explosive air pop from the man's lungs. The Knoug went over backwards, down hard.

The other one roared an oath.

PARR walked on the fallen one's face. He stomped the face and it gurgled. He stomped again in fury as all his frustration and new bitterness found an outlet. He locked the other Knoug in mental battle, but the mind he met was strong, catching him off guard.

The Knoug dove for the huge comset to warn the Fleet.

Parr could hear, from the receiver of the dangling phone, the Commander saying over and over again, "What the hell's going on? What the hell's going on?"

Parr brought the remaining Knoug to his knees with a mental assault.

Parr backed toward the door. As he fought mentally, he managed to slide the force bar across it: They'd play hell getting him out, at least.

His enemy was down, quivering. Parr panted desperately, and then from beyond the door, he felt the growth of mental assault force. Three minds hurrying toward him! Two more minds came in and he staggered and almost fell.

Then he was down, as if from a hammer blow to the chin. He fought, sickened. He began to crawl toward the control board. And fighting, he struggled up, as if under a great weight. New minds came in. And still he could fight. But he was almost down again.

(Five minutes, he thought.)

He found the right lever, pulled. There was the crackle of the heterodyne mind shield. And the control room was isolated by a high, shrill whine. He winced, recovering, and smiled inwardly at the careful devices Knoug officers had to protect themselves against a mutinous crew.

He dampened all the thrust engines with three hacking strokes at knife switches, being careful to get the right ones. He ripped out the engine room control. The Advanceship was dead in space for at least an hour.

HE staggered to the comset. He stumbled over the dead Knoug and kicked the body. He shattered the transmitter with a furious blow.

With fumbling fingers he ripped away the seal the Commander had placed on the receiver. He snapped the volume control to the right. The radio whined.

Someone was trying to call the Advanceship, and Parr smiled grimly.

Another circuit broke in on the call. "Their commander is questioning the advancemen they brought up, I imagine. Let him go. The information we got from the Texas advanceman supercedes it anyway."

Parr cursed monotonously.

"Forward bank in!" another circuit reported.

"Nine stations on planet shield. Ready?"

There was crackling of readiness.

"We'll hit before it. Try to get it set in fifteen minutes."

"In position, there. Eight, back a little."

"Clear hulls. Unscreen."

"Check... Check..."

Parr glanced at his watch. The hour had only minutes of life. What was wrong with Lauri?

"Ready around?"

The Fleet was getting ready to move. Parr screamed in wild frustration.

At the door, the force field was beginning to show strain. Outside they had a huge force director focused on it. Parr speculated idly how they had managed to get it up from the engine room so quickly. The force field at the door began to peel. In a few minutes it would shatter and the control room would be an inferno with every switch and bit of metal melted into smoking blobs.

SHE was searching the shops, kicking in glass, when necessary to gain entrance. She was listening, now, and time dribbled away. Standing amid broken glass, she cocked her head hoping to hear the whisper of the still active comset.

Ten minutes.

What had been wrong with her logic? Why hadn't Kal's body been in one of the four buildings? Even as she searched on she reviewed it in her mind, until suddenly, with an abrupt snap she knew that she had overlooked one. There were not four possible buildings but five.

Kal might have been hiding in the hotel itself!

Nine minutes.

And how many front rooms were in the hotel? A twelve storied welter of windows, and he might be behind anyone.

Nine minutes.

Automatically she was running for the hotel.

(Not the lower floors, she thought, or the Oholos would have had him sooner. They must have come down and then gone back up or else the whole time element was wrong.)

One of the upper floors then?

She would have to chance that.

She was in the deserted lobby. As she ran across it she marveled at the panic of a few hours ago. She saw a busy looter in the shadows, and there were not, certainly enough soldiers to be everywhere.

In her headlong rush she did not see the human form on the second landing before she crashed into him. She gasped as the breath went out of her lungs.

The man reached out for her. "What happened?" His voice was desperate. "I've been asleep, and all of a sudden, when I wake up—"

"Let me go!"

"What happened?" he said pathetically. "The city's so *still.*"

She pushed him back and continued up the stairs.

He ran after her. "Wait!"

At the top floor she saw no exit to the roof.

The corridor was "U" shaped, the bottom of the "U" facing onto the street. Six rooms on it.

"Young lady!" the man cried, rounding the corner of the stairs below her. She dropped her mental range into a low register and struck toward him. But she could not quite find his range and he shook his head and continued up the stairs. She waited, and when he arrived, she said, "Sorry," and hit him on the chin. He rolled halfway down the short flight of stairs.

She searched the six rooms. All were unlocked and empty, and the doors slammed in her wake.

Nothing.

She gritted her teeth and headed for the stairs and the next floor below.

PARR shattered the glass from the emergency deep space suit. He ripped the suit from the hangar and struggled into it with anxious fingers.

It was a minute after the hour.

He hesitated, holding the helmet in his hands.

The force field at the door was nearly gone. The radio crackled with Knoug attack orders.

And then—with infinite relief—he heard her voice, crackling over the other voices. She sounded short of breath and excited.

"What's that?" someone roared in Knoug, and Parr realized they did not understand English, the common language they had used on the planet.

"Idiots!" Parr shrieked. "Fools! Can't *any* of you understand!"

"I'm going to destroy your Advanceship," Lauri said breathlessly. "I am an Oholo. I'm…" Suddenly a Knoug was translating her message.

Last minute instructions to the Fleet ceased.

"I'm going to destroy your Advanceship," she said again. And then, after a breath, she said, "Be careful! Be careful!" And he knew that the last was not to them but to him.

He could wait no longer. The force field was seconds thin. His mind cried desperately, "Hurry!" He clamped down the helmet and all sound vanished.

But her words rang in his mind, "Be careful!" and he was grateful for them. They choked in his throat.

Then he threw the Advanceship into hyperspace.

THERE was a pinwheel of motion that slammed him into the control panel. He could not hear, but everywhere, around him, metal screamed and wrenched and tore.

The force director beyond the door spun loose and sprayed the Knougs around it, and they vanished. It jerked its current cable and was still. A vast rent in the hull let the air whoosh out into hyperspace, and the Knougs all over the Ship puffed and exploded.

Parr came slowly to his senses. He staggered directionless around the control room. Everything was a shambles.

After a while—nearly an hour had elapsed—he was wandering through silent corridors. It was hot inside his suit.

He found the pick-up ships eventually, but they were ripped from their moorings. One seemed upright and serviceable. He tested the motor. The motor worked. He got out and struggled with the escape hatch. Finally it came loose.

He taxied the pick-up ship out of the mother ship.

Hyperspace was grey and hideous. Here and there lights flashed. The vast, battered derelict of the Advanceship lay below him. Hyperspace sped away. He blasted further from the gutted hull and brought up the space shield of his craft. It wavered around him. Behind him the tortured Advanceship exploded.

He hit back toward real space. The craft skittered under his hands as he wrenched at the controls. The motor was strong, but its delicate shielding apparatus had been damaged and there was a sickening jolt. The shield was off and Parr was falling, down, down, down, and lights in his head exploded.

And he thought it was infinitely sad that he had done something decent for the first time and now he was to be punished for all the rest. Then he knew no more...

THE comset had erupted into a babble of incredible confusion after her message. She waited leadenly. She warned the Fleet once more. "If you do not leave at once, we Oholos will destroy your whole Fleet." She had no way of knowing what was happening.

The Knoug commanders, unnerved, cried among themselves:

"No weapon I ever heard of could do *that!*"

"The advanceman was right! They can destroy us!"

"I say we don't stand a chance!"

"Did you hear? It just *vanished.*"

"I'm going to order my ship back."

"I've already shielded for hyperspace."

"What's the Flagship say?"

"What's the Flagship *say?*"

"Commander Cei just pulled out. That makes five."

"As for me, I say, Let's go!"

"The Flagship has already got its hyperspace shield turned on!"

Slowly the voices died away. The comset was silent in Lauri's hand, and she knew that the Fleet had gone. The Advanceship was destroyed.

Remembering Parr, she bowed her head. She saw the body of Kal lying at her feet, where she had found it in the second room on the tenth floor. And she was crying without sound.

CHAPTER ELEVEN

SHE finally got through to the other Oholos. They listened, because the expected attack had not come.

They came for her and she met their airship in the street. They soared above the silent city of Denver.

"A *Knoug!*" one said. "Who ever would have thought a *Knoug* would do that!"

She tried to explain but they did not listen for they were busy with other thoughts. She was still crying, but inwardly now. She said, "Don't you see what he might have *become* within a few years?"

"Imagine hitting hyperspace without a shield," one Oholo said.

"It must have turned the ship inside out!"

"So the Knougs actually believed it was a weapon that did it!" another said, pleased.

Lauri said, woodenly, "He was very strong. He was almost as strong as I am. He would have become even stronger."

"There's no Knoug as strong as one of our best workers, Lauri."

"He was more than a Knoug," she insisted gently. "A Knoug would have just—just gone on being what he was."

She fell silent, remembering.

"It played hell with this planet," an Oholo said. "It'll take years to straighten it out."

"Not years," another said, looking down at the night. "No. I think not years. One of the governments we were primarily concerned with has been changed. The people finally got the chance to overthrow it, and they did. That's a good sign. I think our work will be easier now. It's always easier to rebuild than to change."

Lauri!

She froze. "Listen!"

And they listened, high up.

Lauri!

"Yes!" she cried.

Come to me!

She rushed to the pilot room. She took the controls and spun the ship.

"Did you hear that?" an Oholo said, awed.

"Yes," said another. "...He not only went in unshielded, but he managed to get back!"

They shook their heads.

And within fifteen minutes she had found his ship, lying below in dying moonlight.

SHE brought the aircraft down and within seconds she was running to the wreckage and pulling his limp body from it.

When the space helmet was off his head, he gasped, "Tore hell out of my big ship. And...then I even...up and...wrecked this one, landing...I'm just...damned clumsy."

"Get the surgeon!" Lauri cried.

She held his head in her arms while her lips moved soundlessly. Then she bent to kiss him on the mouth after the Earth fashion, and Parr had never experienced such a sensation of trust and surrender and promise. He let his hand move gently down her arm.

"We'll stay here," she whispered. "We'll stay here and help these Earth people, you and I. You'd like that? To help them?"

"Yes," he said. "It would be nice to...build instead of destroy. It would be nice, I think. You and I could help them. I'd like that."

The surgeon came, and they took Parr out of the suit and after a while the surgeon said, "I don't know much about Knougs. But I'm glad this one is going to be all right."

Lauri laughed hysterically. The tears were open again. "I couldn't kill him," she sobbed.

The other Oholos looked puzzled and polite.

"It's a joke!" she said, dizzy with relief. "Of course he'll live, because even I couldn't kill him!"

Parr smiled up at her.

THE END

POLITICS AND DIVINE MATTERS NEVER MIX...

Life was Marc's oyster. However, things changed radically when subversives shot him; a ghost was ready to haunt his corpse, and Toffee was all set to love him to death!

Things started spinning out of control when Marc stumbled upon the evil plans of a sub-government subversive group. He, of course, felt the need to take immediate action. The bad guys, naturally, also felt the need to take immediate action by "removing" Marc from the equation. Armed with an agile mind and the indefinable spirit of Toffee, Marc set out to face the challenge.

Here is another entry in Charles F. Myers' series of delightful sci-fi fantasy romps featuring that beautiful, ever confounding, will-o-the-wisp...Toffee.

CAST OF CHARACTERS

TOFFEE
Marc's Pillsworth's imaginary, really hot, redheaded lady-friend. She would love nothing more than to have Marc all to herself.

MARC PILLSWORTH
Shot and unconscious. When he come to—wow. Between the antics of Toffee and George the gunshot was nothing.

GEORGE PILLSWORTH
Spiritual projection of Marc. Umm…yep…he's a ghost. His only desire—to see Marc dead!

CONGRESSMAN ENTWERP
This guy is one shady politician—go figure. Will his velvet tongue be enough to save his own hide?

THE THUG
Bodyguard for the Congressman, he's sent to "take care" of Marc. But really now…how many times ya gotta kill a guy?

JULIE PILLSWORTH
Marc's loving wife, really pretty, too—jeez. What this lady has to put up with is enough to make a wife burn an omelet.

JUDGE CARPER
Defendants, complainants, ghosts—all in his courtroom! How's he gonna explain this fiasco?

NO TIME FOR
TOFFEE

By
CHARLES F. MYERS

ARMCHAIR FICTION
PO Box 4369, Medford, Oregon 97504

*For more information about Armchair Books and products, visit our
website at…*

www.armchairfiction.com

Or email us at…

armchairfiction@yahoo.com

CHAPTER ONE

Somewhere, in a place where time and space didn't exist, grey mists began to seeth and swirl, and withal there was an ominous rumbling. The High Council was almost in session.

In a sense, the High Council was already in session, for the Heads of the Council had developed their intellects to such an inconceivable degree that when a meeting of the Council was imminent they could send their thoughts on ahead of them and get the meeting under way even before putting in an appearance. There was an exchange of views and information long before the Heads accomplished the mundane and troublesome business of materialization. Thus it was that the mists of Limbo now rumbled with thought, counter thought and—on this particular occasion downright aggravation, even before the arrival of the Supreme Head in the vapored chambers. There was an air of foreboding.

Having declined all vanities in the pursuit of the Ultimate Intelligence, the Heads had allowed themselves to evolve into literal representations of their titles. Directing all their energy and development to the brain and its encasement, their bodies had suffered proportionately so that now they were little more than a group of preposterously large craniums, shaggy with cerebration, bearing faces weighted with the ponderous woe of Life, Death, Eternity and other such mental ballast. Five in all, they made up a company to be avoided whatever the cost.

THE Supreme Head cleared his throat and Eternity rattled with phlegmy discontent. Baleful glances were exchanged all around.

"Well," said the Supreme Head, after a pause for attention. "I suppose you all know the reason for this meeting by now?"

The Second Head, a bald party with large ears, nodded sadly, "You say this blighted Pillsworth has gone and got himself shot this time?"

"Precisely," the Supreme Head affirmed. "In a broadcasting studio, if you please. There's simply no keeping that man out of trouble."

"But why should we want to keep him out of trouble?" the Third Head, an elongated customer with eye pouches, wanted to know. "That's hardly our responsibility."

"There's George Pillsworth," the Supreme Head said fatefully. "Surely you haven't forgotten about George?"

A hush fell over the Council, a hush of horror.

"Not George again?" the Second Head shuddered. "We don't have to face him again, do we...?" He looked around

NO TIME FOR TOFFEE!

By Charles F. Myers

Life was Marc's oyster, but: subversives had shot him—a ghost was ready to haunt his corpse—and Toffee was loving him to death!

beseechingly at the others. "After all, Pillsworth's only injured, isn't he? He's not dying?"

The Supreme Head looked for a moment as though he wished he had shoulders so he might shrug them hopelessly. "The vibrations are confused again," he sighed. "I don't know what the interference is around Pillsworth, but the call never comes through clearly. All we know is that he's gotten himself into another mess of some sort and is either dead or dying.

"It seems that the subversives are still strongly active in the United States, and of course Pillsworth couldn't stay out of it like a good citizen. He was approached by some men delegated by government authority to take control of national advertising. The theory was that American advertising could be used as a strong combative propaganda weapon against the enemy propaganda already circulating through the country. A committee was delegated to secure the cooperation of the nation's leading advertising agencies. Naturally, since Pillsworth is the nation's leading advertising executive, they contacted him first."

"Then Pillsworth is a subversive?" the First Head enquired. "That's how he got into trouble?"

"Not at all," said the Supreme Head. "That's just it. Pillsworth wasn't subversive, but the government committee was."

"Eh?"

"Exactly. It turned out that the program was one of the cleverest propaganda schemes ever devised. Actually, their aim was to insert alien ideals into the nation's advertising."

"But you said the plan had government approval."

"That's the really clever part of it. The method of presentation, while seeming on the surface to denounce the foreign creed and uphold the American one, actually was designed to win support for the enemy. The sales psychology employed was of the negative."

"Negative?"

"That's correct. It's the old principle of telling people they don't want a thing until they develop a feeling of defiance and decide they are going to have it. It's an extremely subtle approach, but almost infallible if properly developed. Knowing this, these men had a perfect plan, so subtle that even the government didn't recognize it. Also, they had help from within. A certain Congressman Entwerp pushed through the legislation."

"But Pillsworth saw through it?"

"INSTANTLY," the Supreme Head nodded. "It was a principle he had been using assiduously for years, in fact the very one through which he achieved his success. The whole plot was as clear as a May morn the moment he heard it. That's when the trouble started. He contacted Congressman Entwerp."

"Oh, dear!"

"Indeed. Entwerp responded by holding Pillsworth up to ridicule."

"But Pillsworth had logic on his side."

The Supreme Head smiled tolerantly. "That's the Earth for you every time," he said. "Show a human a bit of logic and he gets truculent on the spot. Pillsworth was denounced as a witch hunter and instructed under penalty of law to co-operate to the fullest."

"Shocking," the Third Head said. "I begin to feel sorry for this Pillsworth."

"Pillsworth was similarly shocked. But he didn't feel sorry for himself. Despite his inclination for the quiet conservative life, he fought back."

"Good," the Fourth Head put in. "I'm glad; it gives the story zip."

"My thought in telling you this," the Supreme Head said caustically, "is merely to inform, not entertain."

"Sorry, sir."

The Head nodded acknowledgment. "But to get on, Pillsworth presented his case to a news broadcaster and asked to be allowed to recite his story to the nation in the interests of national security. He was shot. By whom we do not know; the fellow got away. But the fact we must hold in mind is that he definitely was shot."

"Then it really is serious," the Third Head said. "We may have to interview this deadly George after all."

"It's unavoidable," the Supreme Head sighed. "There's no way around it."

"But we're not positive Pillsworth is dead yet. Couldn't we wait and be sure?"

"His vibrations have been broken," the Supreme Head said. "Actually we have no cause to hesitate." He sighed. "I suppose we might as well get it over with."

The others nodded in reluctant agreement. There was an oppressive silence.

"But didn't we banish George?" the First Head said. "We must have after his last excursion to Earth."

"That's right," the Second Head agreed. "I remember distinctly. He attempted to fire poor Pillsworth off into outer space without a pressure suit. We banished him to the Void to sing bass in the Moaning Chorus."

"We certainly picked the right party for the job," the First Head reflected. "There isn't a more base spirit in all Limbo. Has he been summoned?"

THE Supreme Head coughed regretfully. "I issued the call through Message Center before I announced the council."

"Oh, dear," the First Head murmured, "then the stinker is practically on the sloop at this very moment."

"The stinker is crossing the sloop even now," the Supreme Head amended; his gaze fastened hauntedly on a disturbance in the outer mists. "Here he comes."

"Secure your valuables," the Second Head said morosely. "And keep your hands in your pockets."

Hesitantly, under the unblinking disapproval of the Council, George materialized. As the Council watched, a duplicate of Marc Pillsworth's long, lean body, made vague by misted robes, rose solidly out of the moiling vapors. It grew to full stature, rounded out at the shoulders, extended a neck, then stopped short of the head. There was an expectant pause, but nothing further developed.

"The rotter's ashamed to face us," the First Head observed sourly.

"Little wonder," the Third Head muttered. "After the way he's blotted the haunting profession, he hasn't got a leg to stand on."

"George Pillsworth," the Supreme Head intoned with exasperation, "spiritual projection of the mortal entity, Marc Pillsworth, approach the Council. And put on your head, you fool."

George stirred, and his head, working from the chin upward, materialized, revealing the face of Marc Pillsworth. All in all, as faces go, Marc's—and consequently also George's—hit very close to average. It was a nice face, a pleasant face, for all its lack of distinction. On George, therefore, it was a misleading face. With its lean plainness, its serious grey eyes and its shock of sandy hair, it failed utterly to express even a whit of George's unprincipled temperament.

"Is that better, sir?" George asked, edging warily forward.

"Hardly that," the Supreme Head groused. "The less of you the better. However it helps us somewhat to get a clue to the inner festerings of that depraved mind of yours." He gazed at George for a long, reflective moment, then made a sad, clucking sound. "I simply cannot imagine what Marcus Pillsworth must have thought when he discovered that his spiritual entity was a tacky, ebony-hearted, feather-headed wretch like you. Why aren't you more like your mortal source?"

George shrugged sheepishly. "I guess I'm just no damn good," he murmured.

"You flatter yourself," the Supreme Head said. "You're much worse than no damn good. You're simply awful. I wonder if Limbo will ever live you down."

"I hope so, sir," George said contritely.

"Nevertheless," the Supreme Head went on, "much as I loathe it, I suppose we must get on with it. I suppose you know why you've been summoned?"

George nodded dimly. "They reported me for teaching the Moaning Chorus to syncopate."

"What!" the Supreme Head gasped. "You did *what?*"

GEORGE looked up, affrighted; he'd given himself away again with no need. "Yes sir," he sighed resignedly, "I thought that if we got up a good hot act we might be able to wangle a few guest shots with the Celestial Choir. Actually, we've worked out a really sock arrangement of the *Wham Bam Blues*. I'm sure that if you heard it…"

"No!" the Supreme Head roared. "You *couldn't!* Of all the unmitigated…!" He stopped and waited for his spleen to subside. "George Pillsworth," he said, "you are insufferable."

"I suppose so, sir," George said. "However my intentions…"

"Blast your intentions!"

"Yes, sir. I'm very sorry."

"Never mind. In that case it's probably just as well that things are as they are. It'll be a great relief to be rid of you."

"Rid of me?" George said fearfully. "You aren't going to…?"

"Unfortunately, no," the Supreme Head sighed. "What I mean is that your mortal part, Marc Pillsworth, has got himself shot."

George looked up sharply. His whole aspect changed; his eye brightened; his entire being grew more alert. "I'm to be sent to Earth as a permanent haunt? Oh, Sir…!"

"Hold it!" the Supreme Head snapped. "Don't go into a spring dance. There's a hitch."

"Oh," George said, but his eagerness was not noticeably dampened.

TOFFEE **MARC PILLSWORTH**

To George, the merest prospect of a visit to Earth was only to be regarded with rapturous anticipation. To him that distant world of mortals was a place of boundless and exquisite attraction. It was made up in equal parts of liquor, women and larceny and anything else that existed there was merely the result of these things brought together in odd combination. For George, Earth was absolutely the last gasp.

Of course George had never achieved the ultimate accomplishment of establishing permanent residence on Earth, for on all of his previous visits he had arrived only to find that Marc was still alive and that he could not legitimately remain. If on these occasions, George had done his level best to rectify this error with whatever murderous means at hand, it did not imply that the ghost held any personal animosity for Marc. It was simply that George's was the sort of temperament, which boggled at almost nothing to achieve its end.

"What's the catch?" he asked.

"Don't be flip," the Supreme Head admonished. "And stop syncopating."

NO TIME FOR TOFFEE

"Syncopating?" George asked innocently. "I'm standing perfectly still."

"It's your mind," the Supreme Head said. "It's jogging about like a cat on hot bricks. It shows all over you. This is an occasion of enormous seriousness."

GEORGE did his best to assume an expression of profound sobriety. "Yes, sir," he murmured.

"First of all," the Supreme Head continued, "as usual there is some question as to Pillsworth's actual status. He has been shot, it's true, and his vibrations are definitely broken. However, experience has taught us to be wary in the case of Pillsworth. Often we have acted on false alarms in the past and have been sorry." The Head paused and beetled his brow. "Of course we need not have regretted those errors had you behaved yourself at all in the manner of a decent, self-respecting shade. Nevertheless, we don't dare take a chance despite our reluctance in the matter. Pillsworth's wound falls into the mortality class, so we have no alternative but to issue you your travel orders and the usual allotment of ectoplasm." He fixed George with an unhappy stare. "And get that look of evil delight off your face."

"Sorry, sir," George said.

"And make up your mind right now that this is a business trip. If Pillsworth is not dead or definitely dying when you arrive you will return instantly. Do you understand?"

"Yes, sir."

"And if he isn't dead or dying you will do nothing to alter this state of affairs. You will not undertake on your own initiative to shove him off tall buildings, under moving trucks or into open manholes. You will not threaten him with ropes, guns, explosives, rare poisons or knives, or attempt to dispatch him to heaven by means of rocket. Have you got all that straight?"

"Yes, sir," George said quietly. "Hands off. I understand."

"I hope you do," the Head said ominously, "for your own sake. Anyway, I suppose you'd better go along now and start checking out through Supply. All that's left here is for you to raise your right hand and swear by memory to the Ten Commandments of the Hunter's code. However, I suppose you've got them all cribbed on the sleeve of your robe."

George lowered his gaze. "Yes, sir," he murmured. "I have."

"Then skip it," the Head sighed resignedly. "Just clear out."

"Yes, sir," George said, brightening. "Thank you, sir."

As the mists swirled up around George, and he gradually dissolved into their vaporish currents, a joyous grin lighted his face...

CHAPTER TWO

THREE sets of eyes fastened clinically on the X-ray with worried, professional interest.

"There's a slight chance," the first doctor said, "if we operate immediately."

"Too slight," the second murmured. "The bullet's too close to the heart. He'll die on the table."

"He'll die anyway. We're merely taking the only chance there is."

"I suppose so. Has his wife arrived yet?"

"She's with him now."

"He's not conscious, is he?"

"No, certainly not, but they could not keep her away."

"We'd better explain how it is. We're almost certain to lose him."

"I suppose so."

There was a pause before they turned and reluctantly left the room. Outside, in the hospital corridor, the first doctor proceeded to the door at the end of the hall while the other two stayed behind. He opened the door and quietly stepped inside.

Marc lay still on the bed, his pleasant face drawn and pale against the pillow. Julie sat beside the bed, a classic figure of silent grief, her blond, beauty drained with uncomprehending fright. She did not cry. Nor did she move as the doctor walked toward her from the door.

"Mrs. Pillsworth…" the doctor said, but Julie remained motionless. He moved closer to her and placed his hand gently on her shoulder. "We've just seen the X-ray." At this Julie looked up. "We'll have to operate instantly. The preparations are being made now." He paused. "The chances for success are negligible."

Julie nodded dazedly. "I know," she whispered. "I know…"

She did not resist as the doctor took her arm and guided her to the door. At the last moment, though, she paused and looked back at the lean face on the pillow.

"He looks so peaceful," she said. "He looks so content. Does a dying man ever dream, doctor?"

EVEN Marc himself could not have fitted a positive answer to Julie's question. Did he dream? Or had he merely retreated from the world to a realm of absolute reality? He didn't know himself.

He remembered passing through caverns of roaring darkness, only to be caught up by a tongue of searing flame and hurled into some obscure dimness where it seemed that all the thought, melody, all the remembered sensation of a lifetime writhed about him like vague forms, one interposed upon the other, in unpatterned confusion.

But now these entangled vagaries faded away and suddenly he found himself sitting on a green slope at the outer perimeter of a grove of graceful trees. A blue mist drifted lightly up the far rise to soften the horizon. Marc was no stranger to this place for he had visited it often. He felt no dismay at finding himself again in the valley of his own mind. Indeed, through the last few years, it had become as familiar to him as his own home or office. So had the redheaded minx who found her existence there.

Marc stirred and looked around. The landscape was uninhabited. No lovely, lightly clad figure appeared on the horizon, no lithe form emerged from the groves and ran toward him.

Marc frowned anew over the improbable fact of Toffee. Certainly she existed in his mind, a constant and consistent product of his imagination. That was perfectly easy to understand. The parts of it, though, that he never quite got used to were her periods of existence outside his mind, in the world of actuality.

What Marc had never been able to really comprehend was that his mind could project into the physical world a physical being—to such an extent that her existence was not only apparent to himself but also to everyone else who came within the radius of the mental vibration which produced the girl.

The question in Marc's mind, then, was whether Toffee really existed, was truly real, or whether she was merely an hallucination, a sort of contagious hysteria.

Toffee's personality always got in the way of the answer. The girl was infinitely distracting, from the pert aliveness of her quick green eyes to the fun redness of her lips. Beyond that there was the almost shameful perfection of her supple young body. These things blocked analytical thought. Then, too, there was her unerring instinct for roaring, bounding madness, and her absolute contempt for the logical, the moral or the conservative. Toffee, in brief, was at once brash, embarrassing, impetuous, warm, high-handed, endearing, maddening and completely unforgettable. So to all practical purposes, then, she was real; the matter of Toffee's source was pallidly unimportant next to the vivid fact of Toffee herself.

Marc stretched luxuriously and got to his feet, but as he did so he peered around toward the green obscurity of the forest. There was still no movement, no sound. He frowned quizzically. This wasn't at all usual. Always before Toffee had been there to greet him almost at the instant of his arrival. Another time she would be swarming all over him by now.

HE shrugged and started aimlessly up the rise. At first he climbed unhurriedly, but as he drew nearer the trees his gait quickened. At the outskirts of the forest he found himself pausing to listen, but there was no sound. The feathery branches swayed in silent grace before him. A small concern began to trickle into his mind.

The blue mists broke smoothly before his stride as he entered the cool enclosure of the forest. Again he paused.

"Toffee…?" he found himself calling.

There was no answer.

He shoved ahead, and now there was a sort of anxiety in his step, and he took care not to break the stillness lest Toffee answer. An old feeling of bereavement came over him, though he told himself it was foolish. After all, the girl was entirely imaginary, and a pack of trouble into the bargain. Then suddenly he stopped.

An odd murmuring seemed to come from the left. He moved in that direction, stopped to listen, then hurried on. Ahead he saw a dim lightness sketched through the trees, a suggestion of a clearing obscured by the dense branches. He approached it, parted the foliage and looked out. He stopped short.

Toffee sat in the middle of the clearing, her legs folded under her. Her eyes were closed and one slender hand was pressed to her forehead in an attitude of labored con-centration. Her slight tunic, an emerald transparency at best, did little to conceal the impertinent perfection of her figure. She was leaning forward just a bit, and her flaming hair hung loose over her shoulders. She seemed to be chanting some-thing to herself, though Marc couldn't make it out.

"Toffee…?" he said, and stepped forward to brace himself against the inevitable rush of brash affection.

The girl opened her eyes and looked around hastily.

"Sit down somewhere," she said, "and be quiet."

"Huh?" Marc asked.

Toffee didn't answer. Instead, she closed her eyes, swayed back lightly on her shapely haunches and began the muttered chant anew.

Marc swayed a trifle himself, with astonishment—and perhaps a tinge of disappointment. This wasn't like Toffee at all, not by a long shot. He moved slowly to her side and gazed down at her intent, upturned face.

"Toffee…?" he hazarded.

She didn't open her eyes. Her lips moved. "Molecules," she said.

"What?" Marc asked.

"Molecules," Toffee repeated. "Molecules…molecules…"

"Molecules?" Marc said. "What are you talking about?"

Toffee opened her eyes at this and looked up at him with anxious irritation.

"Please be still," she said. "I've got to think about molecules exclusively. It isn't helping any, your gabbing away in my ear."

"But why?" Marc asked. "What about molecules?"

"Everything depends on them, that's all," Toffee said impatiently. "Now, just…"

"But wait a min—!"

"Quiet," Toffee said. "Don't you realize that you're tottering on the brink of death at this very moment? Me, too, for that matter."

"Death?" Marc asked. "What are you talking about?"

TOFFEE looked at him aghast. "Don't you remember?" she asked. "Have you actually forgotten about being shot in the studio?"

Marc stared down at her in growing horror. A, small, agonized memory screamed out of the dark inner shadows of his awareness.

"Oh, Lord!" he cried. "I'm dying!"

"And if those licensed butchers get to hacking you up, you're a goner," Toffee said anxiously. "I have the inside information. There isn't much time. I've got to concentrate like wild."

"But…!"

"Quiet!" Toffee broke in. "Please be quiet," she closed her eyes again and her lips began to move as before. "Molecules," she murmured.

Marc remained rigid at her side.

Panic rose inside him and filled his throat. His impulse was to turn and run blindly—perhaps back to that dying mortal body—but his terror held him transfixed. Staring down at Toffee, he felt he might go mad in the next moment. In the next moment he was certain he had.

Just in front of Toffee, close to the mossy greenness, he caught sight of a quick flicker of light, a strange disembodied illumination that was at once its own source and product. As he watched it flickered again, grew brighter and became a steady radiance. He glanced back at Toffee, but her face had become fixed and mask-like. Her lips no longer moved.

The radiance grew swiftly, to an almost unbearable brightness. In it there was a cold hard suggestion of metal. Then it began to take form and solidify, Marc blinked as the thing, whatever it was, grew slowly out of the gleaming brilliance.

First a cylinder emerged, about a foot long and four or five inches in diameter. For a moment the object seemed to have completed itself, but then, one at either end, a pair of funnel-shaped openings emerged. These completed, a small, two-way switch arrangement appeared at the top and in the center of the cylinder. After that, the radiance was gone and only the strange instrument remained, lying on the grass before Toffee as though cast there by a careless hand.

"What—!" Marc gasped.

Toffee's perky features relaxed. She opened her eyes.

"Did it turn out all right?" she asked brightly. "Is it finished?"

"Huh?" Marc asked. He pointed. "You mean *that?*"

"Oh, wonderful!" Toffee cried, delighted. "It's rather pretty the way it shines, isn't it?"

"What is it?"

"How should I know?" Toffee said blandly. "Just a gadget. There's never been one before."

"You mean you just developed it out of your mind?"

"Sure," Toffee said. "It's a thought product—like me. Now if it only works right…" Picking up the instrument, she looked at it carefully and nodded with satisfaction. "It should be simple to operate."

"But what's it for?"

"I'll show you," Toffee said. She pointed to a nearby tree. "See that?" Marc nodded. "Keep looking at it."

TURNING to the tree, she held the cylinder toward it; so that one of the, funnels was aimed squarely in its direction.

"Now watch," she said, and pressed the switch.

Marc, staring at the tree in rapt attention, started with surprise. Suddenly the tree was gone with no sign that it had ever been there.

"What…!"

"The next part is more important," Toffee said.

"Next part?" Marc said dazedly. "But where is it? Where...?"

"See there?" Toffee said, and this time she pointed to the center of the clearing. "Watch."

Holding the cylinder so that the opposite end was pointed to the clearing, she pressed the switch in the other direction. Instantly the tree shot into being exactly at the spot she had indicated.

Marc stared. It was the same tree—the one that had disappeared—and yet it was subtly different. It seemed greener now, more alive.

"What happened?" he asked. "What did you do to it?"

"Molecules," Toffee said, smiling. "I broke it down into molecules, then projected it again. The machine absorbed the tree in molecules, compressed them, reconstructed the faulty or destroyed ones, eliminated all harmful matter and retained the count to reestablish it in perfect balance and health. It worked fine."

"My gosh!" Marc said.

Drawing close to him, Toffee twined her arms around his neck with knowing deliberation and drew his surprised face down close to hers.

"I'm going to save your stodgy life with molecules, you skinny old, care-worn wraith," she breathed. "Then you'll be in my pay for the rest of your days. Just keep it in mind later when things begin to happen."

"Huh?" Marc said. "What things?"

"You'll see," Toffee said. "Wow!"

Marc drew himself up stiffly. "Now, look here," he said sternly, "you can just get this wow business right out of your head..."

"And if that doesn't work," Toffee said, "I've been studying hypnotism. I can transfix a snake at fifty yards."

She brushed her cheek lightly against his. "Just think of that, you scaly old reptile."

"Just a second," Marc said. "If you think for one sec—"

But the sentiment was lost as Toffee renewed her hold on his neck and kissed him warmly and at considerable length on the mouth.

"That," she whispered, "is just a token payment in advance. Just wait till the mortgage comes due!"

"Why, you little hussy...!" Marc wheezed. "You haven't the moral sense of a brickbat!"

He stopped short, for suddenly the forest had begun to darken and a sharp wind came alive in the trees. He glanced around, startled, as the earth began to tremble beneath them. Instinctively, he whirled about, looking for an escape from the forest, but suddenly, with a groan of dismay, the world went black, and he was only aware of Toffee's arms closing tight about his neck...

CHAPTER THREE

THE orderly was a pale, antiseptic type. And he was resentful. Wheeling Marc along the hallway toward Surgery, he looked down at the drawn face beneath him with a twinge of pique. He strongly resented the fact that the face was not behaving at all as the face of a true corpse-elect should.

According to the orderly, a dying man had no right to twitch and flutter his eyelids the way this one was doing, let alone showing signs of coming completely to life. It made the orderly nervous and upset.

For a moment the orderly almost succumbed to an impulse to walk off and leave the patient to shift for himself. It was what he deserved if he was going to act that way. Nonetheless, he remained. Consequently, Marc's first vision, upon returning to consciousness, was of a pale, fretful face with white eyelashes and thin lips. He had expected something better.

"Who are you?" he asked weakly. "Are you the doctor?"

The orderly shook his head sullenly, "I'm the orderly. The doctor's waiting."

"They mustn't operate," Marc murmured. "I'll die..." He stopped as a pert face suddenly blurred into view just behind that of the orderly. A slender hand brushed back a wayward lock of red hair. Toffee smiled and winked.

Marc moaned. "Oh, so it's you, is it?" he sighed. "What are you so happy about? I feel awful."

"I'm not happy, sir," the orderly said, mystified. "I'm not happy at all. In fact, if you want the truth..." He paused, and the apprehensive expression of one who detects an unseen presence behind him overtook his face. Very slowly, he turned around.

It would be difficult to say what the orderly expected to find behind him; a fanged reptile might have made a good guess, a slavering fiend another. It is certain, however, judging from his reaction, that on the list of things he did not expect to find, a scantily clad redhead was number one. Toffee, her legs crossed to perfection, the cylinder-like gadget under her arm, sat jauntily on the edge of the cart, smiling a bright greeting. The young man leaped backwards and froze in a transfix of amazement.

"Auk!" he exclaimed.

Toffee turned to Marc. "Is he doing a bird imitation?" she asked. "Should I applaud?"

"Don't be funny," Marc said feebly. "I feel terrible."

"I know," Toffee said. "I got here just in time."

"For what?" Marc asked apprehensively. "What are you going to do?"

Toffee patted the cylinder. "I'm going to save your life," she said. "Don't you remember?"

Marc looked at her through heavy lids. "That's silly," he murmured. "Just go 'way and let me die in peace."

Unmindful, Toffee leaped lightly to the floor, stood back and aimed the gadget at Marc. "All set?" she said.

"Here!" the attendant said, suddenly recovering the faculty of speech. "What are you doing?"

"Advancing medical science a mile a minute," Toffee said. "Don't interrupt."

"But…!"

TOFFEE placed her hand menacingly on her hip and fixed the young man with a steely eye. "Am I going to have to deal with you?" she asked, "or are you going to button your lip like a good child?"

The orderly spoke no further.

Toffee raised the cylinder, sighting the length of Marc's lean, sheet-covered body. Then she pressed the switch.

The orderly stared, wide-eyed, and repeated his bird imitation. The place where Marc had lain was suddenly as bare as a banquet board after the feast. Where a moment before there had been a long thin man, now there was only a long, thin sheet.

"Hey!" the orderly bleated. "Ho!"

"So long, phrasemaker," Toffee said, and tucking the cylinder under her arm, moved off quickly down the hall and around the corner.

It was just as the orderly observed the last flirt of Toffee's hip that the doctor appeared from the door of the operating room and looked distractedly in his direction.

"Good grief, man!" he said, "haven't you brought Pillsworth with you?"

The orderly started nervously and looked around.

"He…he…he…!" he gibbered. "That is, she…she…!"

He pointed in hopeless confusion down the hall.

"What are you babbling about?" the doctor enquired shortly. "Where is Pillsworth?"

"He… He's gone, sir!" the attendant blurted.

"Gone?" the doctor said. "Where did he go?"

The orderly looked away down the hall. "There was this girl, see…she had red hair and a can…"

"Now, just a minute, orderly," the doctor said measuredly. "If you think you can distract me with the depressing details of your sex life…"

"But you don't understand! She was holding this thing…and she told me to shut up…and then Mr. Pillsworth wasn't there any more. That's the truth!"

"Let me impress it upon you," the doctor said, "that this is a very serious incident. I can't imagine how a half-dead patient managed to get away from you, but you'll find him instantly and deliver him to surgery if you know what's good for you. Meanwhile, I'll have the alarm sent out to all the wards and offices. I hope you realize that your carelessness has undoubtedly cost the patient his last chance for life. Without the slightest doubt I can pronounce Marc Pillsworth dead right now."

As the doctor spoke these last words, a small gust of wind—or at least what could easily have passed for a small gust of wind—eddied around the corner at the end of the hall. It was this slight disturbance which marked the arrival of George on Earth.

At the sound of the doctor's voice, the ghost stopped, listened, then clasped his hands together in a transport of joy. He had arrived, just in time to receive the happy news! Marc was dead and he, George, had at last secured his permanent residency on Earth. Out of sheer exuberance the delighted spectre let out a little moan of delight.

The orderly, who was watching the doctor gloomily out of sight, turned sharply.

"Mr. Pillsworth?" he quavered thinly. "Mr. Pillsworth, please…?"

CHAPTER FOUR

MEANWHILE Toffee had progressed busily along the corridors of the hospital in search of some private—and preferably secluded—place in which to reconstruct Marc. Finally, rounding a corner, she found herself abreast of a pair of swinging doors and started toward them. She stopped, however, and turned in retreat as the doors suddenly parted and a doctor and nurse, deep in conversation, came into view. She started back the way she had come, but was stopped again by an approaching nurse pushing an elderly female patient in a wheelchair flanked on either side by a crutch. Looking for an avenue of escape, Toffee spotted a white linen screen against the wall and darted quickly behind it to bide her time till the traffic had subsided.

This ruse, on the face of it, hadn't a flaw and should have worked like a charm. It should have that is, if Toffee, in her haste, hadn't plumped against the wall and unknowingly pressed the button of the gadget.

The result of this little accident was that the doctor and the nurse approaching from one direction, and the nurse and the patient coming from the other—all four of them suddenly found themselves confronted by a tall, thin man standing bewilderedly in the center of the hall with nothing to grace his long frame but an extremely brief linen shift loosely attached at the back. Toffee had released Marc into reality and good health, but costumed only for the operating table.

No one was more acutely aware of this deficiency than Marc himself. Looking around unhappily at his stunned beholders and taking in his slight coverage all in a single glance, he was taken with a seizure of shocked modesty.

Hunkering down into a squat he clutched the hem of his gown desperately to his knees.

"My word!" the elderly patient said, leaning forward in her chair. "What in the world does that man think he's doing!"

"I don't like to think," the nurse said, looking away. "It's bound to be something disgusting."

"Here you!" the doctor called from the other end of the corridor. "You can't do that! Why are you crouched down in that obscene way?"

"I'm naked!" Marc wailed. He lowered his voice to a whisper. "I'm downright exposed!"

"There's no reason to whisper about it," the doctor said nastily. "We can all see."

"Oh, my gosh!" Marc cried. Looking around for a retreat, his frantic gaze fell on the screen. Still in a squat, he hobbled swiftly toward it.

"Look at him!" the patient cried, rising slightly in her chair. "Here, you! Stop doing that, for heaven's sake! You look like an ailing duck!"

"That's nothing to what I'd look like if I stood up," Marc panted in one last sprint for the screen. "That would be worse."

IT was not until this point in the proceedings that Toffee began to realize what had happened. Listening to the voices in the hall, it had struck her that one of them had a dreadfully familiar ring to it. It was much to her dismay that, in peering around the edge of the screen, she suddenly found herself practically eyeball to eyeball with Marc. She let out a small, strangled cry.

"Oh, my gosh!" she said.

"For Pete's sake, let me in there!" Marc said.

"But how did you get out there?"

"How should I know? Never mind that, let me in. They're all looking!"

"At what?"

"I shudder to think. Please let me in!"

"But why are you all doubled up like that?"

Tired of words, Marc reached up to the screen to pull it away so he could get behind it. Unfortunately, it was at this same instant that Toffee decided to shove it open to make room. With their combined efforts, the screen buckled, folded, teetered and fell, cracking Marc solidly on the head. The next moment found him in an unconscious sprawl on the floor. The area behind the screen was starkly deserted. The observers crowded in swiftly to see what had happened.

"Good God!" the doctor cried, staring down at Marc. "It's Pillsworth, the man they're looking for in Surgery!"

"Is he dead?" the nurse asked.

The doctor shook his head. "He's breathing. Run and call an orderly to take him along instantly. Hurry!"

As the nurse hurried off, the elderly patient removed one of the crutches from the side of her chair and passed it experimentally through the vacant area beyond the screen. She shook her head in perplexity.

"By golly," she said, "I could have sworn he was talkin' to somebody back there."

CHAPTER FIVE

WHILE this untimely denouement was rounding out in the hallway, a mad drama of another sort was beginning to ferment in the Pharmacy.

Olliphant Gunn, the rotund and habitually foggy keeper of the dopes and drugs, had been watching it for several minutes; there was trouble brewing in the Salts and Syrups—trouble of a most mysterious and upsetting nature. The containers, for all the world as though they had suddenly been endowed with some idiotic life of their own, had begun to shift about all by themselves. Watching a jar of salts hurl itself to the floor and splash its contents out in a whitish mess, Olliphant Gunn concluded definitely that there was some sort of flimflam afoot.

This conclusion was stoutly strengthened as he witnessed the progress of his private bottle from its hiding place amongst the medicants to a position in mid-air in front of the shelves. Olliphant began to quiver about the dewlaps. He quivered even more as the bottle uncapped itself, tilted upward and emptied a noticeable portion of its contents into—into absolutely nothing at all!

Olliphant fell back in his chair, slack of jaw, and it is doubtful, had anyone been able to apprise him of the truth of the matter, that he'd have felt any better about it. To a man in his cups, as Olliphant was, the news does not come lightly that he is in the company of a thirsty ghost, with an unerring nose for whiskey, and a predisposition for celebration.

Olliphant watched in bleary disbelief as the bottle repeated the tilting and emptying process. Then his mood began to change. Regardless of what this obviously demented bottle thought it was up to, it had no right to deplete his private reserves in this callous fashion. The slack jaw of Olliphant Gunn hitched itself up and became firm.

"Stop that!" Olliphant roared. "You stop that right now, damnit!"

For a moment the bottle wavered, as though startled, then defiantly upended a third time and brought the lever of the coveted liquor down still further. Quite as though to rub salt in the wound, it burped with grandiose satisfaction.

"Damnation!" Olliphant gasped. "I'll teach you, you blathering bottle!"

Heaving his considerable bulk up out of his chair, he hurled himself bodily toward the object of his wrath.

THE laws of nature, however, were against Olliphant from the very beginning. As the bottle darted out of his reach, sheer momentum carried him headlong into the dim reaches of Salts and Syrups. Gravity delivered him along with a quantity of gummy liquid and gritty crystallines to the floor. Settled in a sticky puddle of wreckage, Olliphant glanced around with a reddish, enraged expression. Besides salt and syrup, there was blood in his eye.

At a distance sufficiently out of reach, yet insultingly near, the bottle was bobbing about amusedly. Indeed, Olliphant distinctly heard a soft chuckling sound coming from its direction. With a jungle roar he surged up from the floor and launched a second attack. This netted him another disastrous collision, this time with the glassware department. The Pharmacy was swiftly being transformed into a scene of chaos.

In the interval, the bottle had retreated to a position by the doorway and was humming maddeningly to itself. Suddenly it burst into full-throated song.

"Goin' to Louisiana," it warbled, "for a case of good whis-kee! Goin' to Louisiana with a hussy on mah knee!"

Olliphant settled himself sadly on an untidy mound of rubble and began to brood. There was no use denying it; the thing was just too much for him. As he watched the bottle bog back and forth in time with the idiot song, a large tear trickled down his cheek. Olliphant Gunn was just a broken reed in the holocaust of Life, and his ruination had come about through a mere mad bottle. The man began to blubber hopelessly.

It was during this heart-rending climax that the nurse, a small blonde, appeared at the doorway and stared into the pharmacy with large wondering blue eyes.

The invisible George, who had been enjoying his own singing to the utmost, stopped at the sight of the newcomer in mid verse. Things, he decided, were beginning to look up. Warmed by the liquor, George was dazzled and enchanted.

Unfortunately the nurse was neither of these. Striding through the door, she stepped into a trickle of syrup and skidded dangerously toward Olliphant. George, feeling that things were moving in the wrong direction entirely, seized upon the floundering blonde with one deft swoop of his invisible arm and lifted her to dry ground. It was a moment before he was able to account for the girl's shrill screams.

A period of stupefied silence followed as the nurse glanced around suspiciously. As a girl who, in line of business, had experienced considerable traffic with men, she was disposed to know to the exact moment when she had been forcibly clutched by a masculine hand. Also, which only made matters worse, she was a girl who knew where she had been clutched and why.

IN looking around for masculine hands available for clutching, a quick survey told the nurse that the room inventoried two and both of them were the exclusive property of Olliphant Gunn. Geographically it seemed impossible that either of these hands could have performed the recent clutching, but in her anger the nurse was not the one to quibble over details. Seizing up a large crystal beaker she unhesitatingly smashed it to splinters on Olliphant's skull with one smart whack. Olliphant looked up through his tears.

"What you wanna do that for, lady?" he sobbed.

"You know what for," the nurse gritted, looking around for further ammunition. "And that's only the beginning. If you ever..." She stopped as she suddenly encountered the floating bottle. Instinctively, or perhaps out of sheer surprise, she grabbed for it. At any rate, it was not until she had gotten a grip on the thing that she realized that this was a bottle not properly on the up and up. This fact was brought home to her even more clearly when the bottle refused to budge in her grasp and even showed a definite tendency to pull away.

For a long moment the nurse merely stared at the bottle with a wondering gaze. Then slowly an expression of determination came into her pretty face. Squaring her stance, she took hold of the offending container with both hands.

"It's no use," Olliphant said from the floor. "That bottle's mean."

Heedless, the nurse braced herself and tugged with all her strength. The bottle gave by a foot, then lurched drunkenly in her grasp. Down on the floor the rivulet of syrup became disturbed, as though feet were churning through it desperately seeking to regain lost traction.

Suddenly the bottle gave way and the nurse toppled backwards into Olliphant's lap. Olliphant received this new burden with resignation and a grunt. Across the room, however, there was another sound, as of a body coming in swift contact with the floor.

"Damn!" the nurse said hotly, turning to Olliphant. "Keep your big oafish hands off me! Stop reaching."

"I'm only reaching for the bottle," Olliphant said. "It's mine."

"It didn't feel like it," the nurse retorted. "It felt more like…" She hesitated as from the corner of her eye she caught a glimpse of a long body sprawled on the floor. At first glimpse it seemed that the body had no head, but as she looked more closely she saw that it did, though she had the peculiar sensation that it had just come into being. Handing Olliphant the bottle she got to her feet and approached the prone figure. Noting that it was dressed for surgery, she stood staring down at it quizzically for a moment.

"Holy smoke!" she breathed. "It's Pillsworth!" She turned to Olliphant. "Come on and help me. We've got to get him down to Surgery right away!"

CHAPTER SIX

MARC felt himself rising through the last shredded mists of unconsciousness. He tried to open his eyes but a glaring light made the attempt too painful.

"Give him the anaesthetic," a voice said close by.

Panic pulsed through Marc's body. They were going to operate! Necessity gave him a surge of strength and he sat up, staring wildly at the three doctors gathered over him.

"No!" he said. "Don't! I'm all right!"

"Lie down, Mr. Pillsworth," the doctor nearest advised. "Just lie down and it will all be over within a minute."

"But I'm all right!" Marc said desperately. He glared around at the nurse holding the mask for the anesthetic. "Get away from me!"

"Hysteria," the doctor said. "Quite understandable after what he's been through. He'll have to be restrained."

The other two nodded in agreement. Watching Marc closely, they took up positions on either side of him. The first doctor moved to a place at Marc's feet.

"When I give the signal," he whispered, "we'll all grab at once."

"I heard that!" Marc yelled. "Stay away from me, you croakers, or I'll...!"

"Okay!" the doctor cried. "Grab!"

The scene over the operating table, for a moment thereafter, was a living abstraction in flailing arms and legs. Though Marc managed at one point to insert his thumb into the eye of the first doctor and his foot into the mouth of the second, the odds were too great against him. In the end he found himself pinioned helplessly to the table.

"All right, nurse," the doctor said, "fit the mask to his face. As soon as the body's relaxed…"

"You leave that body alone," a pert feminine voice said tartly. "That body happens to belong to me, for what it's worth, and I don't want it tampered with. I particularly don't want it relaxed. I want it alert and twitching in every fiber and if you don't leave it alone I'm going to lay into the bunch of you bare fisted!"

A tense silence overtook the group around the operating table. The doctors looked at each other, then turned to observe the dismaying redhead who had mysteriously appeared, just behind them.

"How did you get in here?" the first doctor said uncertainly.

"I'm the owner of that body you are flinging about there," Toffee said hotly, shifting the gadget under her arm and placing a hand on her hip. "That body's mine right down to the last molecule and I've come to fight for it if I have to."

MARC sat up under the relaxed grips of the doctors, his face scarlet. "Why do you have to go around telling people things like that?" he asked plaintively.

"I could put it another way," Toffee said. "Dirtier. For instance…"

"No!" Marc cried. "It's dirty enough already."

The doctor turned to Marc. "Who is this woman?"

"I don't know," Marc lied quickly. "I've never seen her before in my life. Why don't you throw her out of here?"

"Why, you lying old ingrate!" Toffee flamed. "For two cents I'd climb up there on that table and perform a few operations of my own!"

"Madam!" Marc said distantly, "whoever you are, do you really think you ought to take on in public in this brazen way?"

"I'll take you on in public, no holds barred, you thin-nosed phony," Toffee gritted. "You don't know what brazen is yet!"

The doctor turned to the nurse. "Call the orderlies and have this woman removed," he said. "And have them give her a blanket or something to wear. We can't delay the operation another moment. I'll give the anesthetic myself."

"Hey!" Marc yelled. "Toffee…"

"Go ahead, doctor," Toffee said with evil satisfaction. "Rip him open. Slit him from ear to ear and top to bottom, I won't lift a finger."

"No!" Marc cried. He turned to Toffee in panic. "It'll mean the end of both of us!"

"Pardon my girlish laughter," Toffee said. "It's worth it, dogmeat, to see you get yours after the way you've treated me. Either you fork over that lanky frame of yours, or you're going to be out of frames entirely. That's the way it stacks up."

"Do you have to be so vulgar about it all?" Marc asked weakly. "With all this talk about bodies and frames, I'm beginning to feel like just so many soup bones displayed on a counter."

"That's exactly the parallel I've been searching for," Toffee said complacently. "In fact if there's anything vulgar in all this, it is your body. Come to think of it, it suddenly strikes me as so vulgar I'm no longer interested in it."

"Please!" Marc cried as the doctors gripped him to the table. "Use that gadget of yours—anything! Please!"

"Sorry, son," Toffee said. "I guess you'll remember after this never to forget a lady's name."

Marc looked up and saw the mask bearing down toward his face, "Toffee!" he yelled, "For Pete's sake!"

THE mask miraculously paused in its descent, stopped. The action around the table came to a sharp halt. Eyes swiveled toward the door. Marc turned on his side just in time to observe Olliphant Gunn lumbering into the room under the weight of George's upper quarters.

The nurse, her blond hair in a state of dishevelment, followed bearing the feet and legs. Arriving at a position inside the door, they deposited their burden on the floor where it instantly curled over on its side and emitted a sodden snore.

"It's Mr. Pillsworth," the nurse said breathlessly, shoving back her hair. "We brought him straight down without waiting for the orderlies." She looked up into the stunned faces staring back at her from around the table. Then her gaze fell to Marc.

"My God!" she gasped.

"Good Lord!" Marc groaned, taking in the stupid, smiling face of George.

"Jesus!" breathed the doctor.

"Amen," Toffee put in glibly. "Who's taking up the collection?"

Marc turned to Toffee. "It's that gosh-awful spook again!" he breathed. "He would have to show up now!"

"Actually," Toffee said, "he could not have shown up at a better time. I really was going to help you out, but now we have George."

Marc's eyes brightened with slow realization. "Of course," he said, then turned as he felt the doctor's hand on his shoulder. "Yes?"

"Mr. Pillsworth," the doctor said tensely. "You are Mr. Pillsworth, aren't you?"

Marc smiled with hypocritical innocence. "No," he said. "That's what I've been trying to get through your thick skull." He pointed to George. "That's Pillsworth there on the floor.

And if you ask me he's in a pretty critical condition. You'd better start sawing away at him right now before he pops off of natural causes and robs you of the sport."

"Oh, my word!" the doctor gasped. "How can I ever tell you...!"

"Come," Marc said grandly, turning to Toffee, "let's leave this blood-splattered slaughter house."

"I'm all for it," Toffee said gaily. "Let's flee."

"I thought you didn't know that woman," the doctor said confusedly.

"'I begin to recognize her now," Marc replied urbanely. "It was my horror at the crass brutality of the medical profession that drove her tender memory from my mind."

"But, I..." the doctor began hopelessly.

"Say no more," Toffee said airily.

"You can tell your side of it in court."

THE two of them, linking arms, started toward the door. They were just about to sweep out of the room when suddenly the situation hit a new snag. It was at this juncture that George opened his eyes, waggled them around woozily, then reared up in a sitting position, staring at Marc.

"You!" he said with a strangled gasp. "You're alive!" The way he said it, it sounded like a hideous accusation.

Marc stopped short, caught off guard. "Of course I'm alive," he said.

"But you can't be!" George wailed, great tears of awful disappointment welling in his eyes. "It isn't fair! You have to be dead!"

"I'm sorry," Marc said, somewhat at a loss. "I'm not."

"It's rotten," George said with drunken bitterness. "It's cruel. I'm probably the only ghost alive who's haunted by a human!"

"Well, it's a distinction," Toffee offered hopefully.

"Just a minute," the doctor put in suspiciously. "What's going on here? What are you people talking about?"

Marc nodded sadly toward George. "The poor chap's delirious," he said. "We're only trying to humor him."

"Oh, yeah?" the doctor said. His gaze moved from Marc to George and back to Marc again. "Just which one of you really is Marc Pillsworth?"

Marc and George pointed at each other in unison. "He is!" they chorused.

The doctor passed a trembling hand over his forehead and lifted his gaze to the ceiling. A tremor of frustration passed through his sturdy frame. He turned to the small blonde.

"Is Mrs. Pillsworth still in the waiting room?" he asked.

"I believe so, sir," the nurse said.

"Will you please call her in here to make an identification?"

"No!" Marc said, glancing uneasily in Toffee's direction. "Don't do that...! I mean there's no need to disturb Mrs. Pillsworth. Obviously this pitiful creature here on the floor is Pillsworth. Just by looking at him you can see he's under the weather."

At this George drew himself up sedately, stiffling a hiccough, "Nothing of the sort," he said piously. "I'm in perfectly splendid condition."

"Go ahead, nurse," the doctor said firmly. "Bring Mrs. Pillsworth."

"Yes, sir," the nurse said, and departed.

"But, you can't afford to delay the operation that long," Marc said. "You said so yourself. Anyone with half an eye can see that this poor man is getting more feeble by the second. You owe it to him to slit him open immediately...!" In speaking Marc had paused to look at George. The result was that the words froze on his lips. Never had he spoken more truly; George was not only getting more feeble but more non-existent by the second. His legs had evaporated to the knees, his arms were entirely gone. Where his eyes should have been there were now only empty sockets. Staring at this awesome demonstration, the doctor tottered slightly and braced himself against the operating table.

"Oh, good Lord!" he moaned.

"Stop that, you coward," Marc said angrily. "Stop sneaking out like that!"

IN response, George merely dissolved his head to a grinning skull. "Gotta go now," he chortled hollowly. "Gotta be corking off." He turned to the others and clacked his teeth menacingly. Olliphant Gunn was the first to snap.

"There's just so much that human flesh and blood can stand," the poor man wailed, and leaping to the operating table he snatched up the anaesthetic mask and plunged it over his face.

"Come on," Toffee said urgently, tugging at Marc's sleeve. "Let's get out of here before that cheap ghost sticks us with an operation."

Marc jolted into action. Under Toffee's guidance, he lunged out the door and started down the hall.

"Let's leave this place," Toffee said. "Let's go somewhere where we can have fun."

"We can't leave like this," Marc said, indicating their brief attire. "We can't go out on the street half naked."

"We can say we're artists' models on our way to work," Toffee said. "Come on."

Marc didn't pause to debate the point as a cry from the operating room indicated that the doctors had recovered from their dismay with an urgent sense of loss.

Together, he and Toffee began to run. They proceeded swiftly around a corner and down a flight of steps to the floor below. Suddenly Marc stopped.

"That's wrong?" Toffee asked.

"Listen," Marc said. "What's that?"

Toffee listened. Descending footsteps sounded on the stairs behind them. She whirled about. The stairway was unoccupied.

"George," she said disgustedly. "He's following us."

The footsteps stopped guiltily.

"Okay," Marc said, addressing himself to the empty stairs. "It's no use pretending you're not there. You might as well show yourself."

A subdued hiccough echoed out of the emptiness, but that was the extent of George's communication.

"If you're entertaining any notion of bumping me off so you can stay here," Marc warned, "just forget it. I'm alive and I intend to stay that way."

"Just ignore him," Toffee said.

"He's bound to get bored and go away if we refuse to pay any attention to him."

CHAPTER SEVEN

THE discussion went no further, for suddenly there were sounds of approaching pursuit from above. Grabbing Toffee's arm, Marc raced ahead, down the hall and around another corner. A third set of footsteps continued to sound in their wake.

"He's still with us," Toffee panted.

"The vulture," Marc said. "He's just hoping they'll catch me. Run faster."

Renewing their efforts, they left behind another stretch of corridor, turned another corner. There they stopped abruptly. Ahead a group of orderlies loomed before them.

"That's them!" a young athletic type yelled. "That's Pillsworth!"

"To hell with Pillsworth!" a companion responded. "Get the dame! She's practically all skin, just like they said!"

Marc and Toffee darted back around the corner.

"Surrounded!" Toffee panted. "I think that sums up the situation."

"What'll we do?" Marc asked confusedly.

Toffee pointed to a door marked JANITOR'S CLOSET. "In there," she said. "Quick!"

They ran to the door, threw it open and darted inside just as their pursuers surged into view at either end of the hallway. They paused in the darkness to listen. As the sounds of the chase continued outside they turned their attention to their new surroundings. The air was close with the heady aroma of cleaning fluid, wax polish and disinfectant.

"Isn't there a light in here?" Toffee asked.

"I can't find one," Marc said. "I've looked all over."

"Well," Toffee said, "at least it's a place to relax for a bit and catch our breath. I just wish it didn't smell so oppressively clean. I was hoping for a bit of dirt tonight—of the right sort, of course."

"You stay on your side of the closet," Marc said, "and I'll stay on mine."

"We'll never get anywhere that way," Toffee said. "Suppose Romeo had taken that attitude with Juliet?"

"They'd both have lived a lot longer," Marc said.

"I suspect that George is in here with us," Toffee said. "I fancy I hear him breathing back there amongst the mops and brooms."

"I suppose he is," Marc said.

There was a pause, followed by a number of rattling sounds. "What are you doing?"

"There's a whole shelf of bottles over there," Toffee said. "I'm just sniffing about to see if there's anything interesting. And there is. The janitor has strong tastes. Irish whiskey, I should judge, by the jolt of it. Have some?"

MARC paused, took note of the new vapors overriding those of the cleaning fluids.

"Well," he said, "it is a little drafty in this nightgown."

Toffee handed him the bottle in the darkness. "Bottoms," she said pleasantly.

"The expression," Marc said sedately, "is bottoms up."

"Up or down," Toffee said, "it doesn't matter. I was just tossing in bottoms at random. Assorted bottoms, so to speak. If you prefer them up, you'll get no argument out of me."

There was a smacking sound as Marc lowered the bottle from his lips. "Let's just skip the bottoms," he said, "and go on to something else."

"Sounds pretty giddy," Toffee mused, "all this leaping about over bottoms. However…"

"Look outside," Marc suggested wearily, "and see if they're still out there."

"Okay," Toffee said. A small shaft of light darted in and out of the closet as she opened the door and closed it again. "They're churning about like cattle in a loading chute," she reported. "Where are you?"

"Sitting on the floor," Marc said. "I'm beginning to find this place restful."

"You're beginning to stink of Irish whiskey," Toffee said. "Stop gulping at that bottle like a great fish and hand it back."

"I wonder if we should offer George a drink?" Marc said with growing amiability. "I definitely heard him breathing back there just now. Sounds a trifle wheezy, I'm afraid."

"I think we ought to banish George from our minds," Toffee said. "Besides, now that I've got the bottle back I don't intend to be free about handing it around for quite some time."

"All right," Marc said. "Have it your way. George is banished."

There was a prolonged period of contented silence, broken intermittently by faint gurgling sounds, first from one side of the closet then the other. It was Toffee who finally spoke.

"By the way," she said, "what was all that nonsense about your getting yourself shot?"

"Oh, that," Marc said negligently.

"It's a bunch of subversives. They have a subtle plan to poison the minds of the public against the government—with the government's permission. I went on the air to expose them, but they had me shot to stop me. There was this dark fellow with a scar over his left eye in the control booth…"

He paused. "Holy smoke! I forgot. This is serious business, isn't it?"

"It sounds like it," Toffee said.

"How far did you get in your broadcast?"

"I didn't even get started. I suppose I ought to try to do it again."

"If they think you're dead or dying, they won't be watching for you any more."

"That's right," Marc said. "Let's get out of here."

"Okay," Toffee said. "Just take your arms away from my waist so I can get up."

"Huh?" Marc said. "I don't have my arms around your waist."

"You haven't!" Toffee said. "Didn't you take the gadget from under my arm either?"

"Of course not."

"It's that sneaky George," Toffee snorted. "And when I think of how I was enjoying it…!" She turned in the darkness. "Let go of me before I lose my temper, George. So help me, you spurious spectre, I'll twist your head off when I get ahold of you."

There was no answer but apparently the threat had taken hold; there were sounds of Toffee getting to her feet.

"That'll hold him," she said. "Look outside and see how things are. I want that gadget back."

Marc fumbled his way to the door, opened it a crack, then shoved it all the way open.

"All clear," he said and turned back to Toffee. "Can you see him back there? Is he visible?"

"I can just make him out," Toffee said, peering into the back of the closet. "He's sort of lurking."

"Okay, you rat," Marc said. "Come out of there and give it to us. Snap into it."

There were shuffling sounds from the shadows and slowly a figure emerged into the light. It was a dark, heavy figure. The face was swarthy and there was a scar over the left eye. The man leered at the two in the doorway.

"Okay," he said. "Keep your shirts on, I'm going to give it to you all right. I'm going to give it to you good."

He moved closer. In his left hand was Toffee's gadget, in his right an enormous revolver.

CHAPTER EIGHT

THE swarthy man closed the door to the storeroom, locked it and shaking his head, moved purposefully down the hallway to a door at the front of the warehouse. He stopped and knocked, and as an unintelligible grunt issued from inside, he opened the door and entered.

"I got 'em," he announced.

Across the room a portly gentleman with a white mane and great shaggy black eyebrows looked up from a sheaf of papers on the desk before him.

"Them?" he said. "I told you just to pick up Pillsworth and finish him off."

The swarthy man glanced away, embarrassed. "I couldn't finish him off congressman. He wasn't even started. I went to the hospital, like you told me, to make sure about Pillsworth—and I was going along the hall lookin' for this place where they cut 'em up—and all of a sudden there was a racket like a lot of people runnin' around and yellin', so I ducked into this closet to keep undercover. Well, I was only in there a little bit when all of a sudden somebody yanks the door open and this guy and this dame come shaggin' in with hardly any clothes on. So I kept quiet and listened."

"I'm not interested in the sordid doings behind the scenes at the hospital," Congressman Entwerp interrupted. "Stick to the pertinent facts."

"Oh, no, it wasn't nothin' like that. I just listened and pretty soon it come up in what they were sayin' that this guy with the dame is none other than Pillsworth himself. And believe me, congressman, I can't explain it, but there ain't a thing wrong with him—physically."

"Physically?" the congressman asked. "What do you mean?"

"The guy's mentally a mess," the thug said. "So's this dame with him. She's a terrific lookin' little job, but crazy as a coot. It's a dirty shame."

"How do you know they're crazy?"

"Just ask Hank. He drove the car. All the way over from the hospital they kept talkin' to this guy who wasn't there, and bawlin' him out for followin' them everyplace. They called him George, and they carried on a regular conversation with him. It was weird, leave me tell you. But one thing, this guy George, whoever he is, is lucky he doesn't exist; the way that little dame kept tellin' him what she was going to do to him if he didn't show himself and help them out of this jam was enough to curl your hair. Pillsworth was all the time tellin' this imaginary character what a ghoul he was to be hangin' around just to see him get killed. They're both nuts, boss, an' no lie!"

"Maybe it was just an act," Congressman Entwerp suggested skeptically.

"I don't think so. You'd really have to feel mean to say some of the stuff those two was dishin' out to this George." The thug paused and withdrew Toffee's thought gadget from his pocket. "Look what I lifted off the dame in the closet." He placed it on the desk before the congressman. "She's plenty hot to get it back. You'd think it was somethin' worth somethin'."

"What is it?"

"I don't know. Some sort of two-way flashlight, I guess. Just a piece of junk."

THE congressman bent his shaggy head close over the gadget and examined it minutely. He picked it up, weighed it in his hand, then shrugged and dropped it negligently into his pocket.

"Let's have a look at these two crackpots," he said, rising from his chair. "We'll have to dispose of them, of course."

"Okay," the thug said. "I just hope they've got things settled with this George before we get there."

Back in the storeroom, however, events were lurching ahead in a most uncertain manner. Things had started with an air of mild strangeness and mounted swiftly to a state of wild-eyed madness.

Finding themselves confined and in the hands of blood-thirsting murderers, Marc and Toffee had paused only momentarily to survey their musty prison, the cases of wines, brandies and whiskies stacked along the walls, before returning to the subject uppermost in their minds. Toffee, doubling her fists, addressed herself to the room at large.

"George," she said evenly, "we know you're with us. You gave yourself away in the car when you let that foot materialize, and you'll give yourself away again. And when you do, brother, I'm going to kick your teeth out one at a time and have them made into shirt studs. I'm going to…!"

"It's no use threatening him," Marc interrupted. "He's got the advantage. He's just hanging around waiting for me to be killed. And he'll probably have his way before they're done with us."

In answer, a stiffled yawn echoed from somewhere in back of them. Toffee whirled about.

"Listen to him!" she fumed. "Now he's rubbing it in! That was the most put-on yawn I ever heard."

She started forward, but Marc put out a hand to stop her. He drew her toward the corner.

"Listen," he said in lowered tones, "I've just thought of something. Maybe we can trap him."

"We certainly should be able to," Toffee agreed hotly. "George is pure rat, through and through. If we only had some cheese…"

"What about whiskey?" Marc asked. "There's plenty of it here, and where George is concerned it's the best bait in the world."

"I wonder why he hasn't been at it already?" Toffee said, surveying the crates along the walls. "The place is practically seething with the stuff."

"He's too smart," Marc said. "He doesn't want to show where he is. By the time he opened a crate and got the bottle out we'd have him located. He's afraid we'd slug him."

"Of course we'd slug him," Toffee said. "I personally intend to bop the living bejesus out of him at the very first opportunity. What difference does that make?"

"He knows what we're after," Marc explained. "He knows we want him to show himself to these people so they won't know which one of us is me. And look what happened to George the last time he was knocked out."

TOFFEE looked up with a smile of understanding. "Of course!" she said. "He lost control of his ectoplasm and materialized."

"Exactly," Marc said, "and it might happen again. Then it would not be just a matter of confusing them with the two of us. If George materialized we could leave him to take the rap all by himself."

"Wonderful!" Toffee said. "Let's do it. It would serve everybody right. How do we trap him?"

"It's simple," Marc said. "We open the crates and get the bottles out for George. At first we pretend to forget about him; we sit around and act like we're swilling down whiskey by the gallon and having the time of our lives. This will drive George close to madness, locked in a room with two drinkers and no drop for himself. When we figure he's sufficiently worked up, we'll weaken and offer him a drink. He won't be able to resist. While one of us hands over his bottle, the other takes a fix on George's position and bashes the daylights out of him with his." Marc permitted himself a smile of pride. "You see?"

"Marvelous," Toffee said. "I particularly love that part at the end, where George gets bashed. Can I be the basher?"

"Okay," Marc agreed. "Let's go. And remember, act as though you've never enjoyed drinking anything so much in your whole life."

With tremendous nonchalance, the two moved across the room to the stacked crates.

"My, my," Marc said in a declamatory, radio announcer's tone, "what do you suppose we have here in all these interesting-looking crates?"

"I should think," Toffee said on cue, "that they contain bottles of fine old tangy whiskey. Of course that's just a random guess, but I believe it's a shrewd one. Shall we have a look?"

"Oh, let's!" Marc cried, with a false grin of eagerness. He turned slightly in what he presumed to be George's direction. "A drink of fine old tangy whiskey would certainly taste mighty good just now."

"I can think of nothing better!" Toffee said, smacking her lips loudly. "My mouth fairly waters!"

Marc reached one of the crates down and, placing it on the floor, pried up one of the slats. He reached out two bottles and handed one toward Toffee.

"Well, well," he cried with studied joviality. "Look what I found!"

Toffee clapped her hands after the manner of a witless child. "Oh, goody!" she gurgled. "Some of that wonderful fine old tangy whiskey! Just what I hoped for!" She took the bottle, opened it and took a swallow. She blanched and covered her face with her hand. "Ugh!" she rasped.

"Yes, sir!" Marc said, lifting his bottle to his mouth. "Some of the finest, oldest and tangiest fine old tangy whiskey there is." He rolled his eyes in broad anticipation. "Yes, sir, bedad!"

"It's a good thing you said that before you tasted the stuff," Toffee hissed between clenched teeth. "You'd never have the breath afterward."

THE warning came too late; Marc had already downed a large swallow. He closed his eyes and gagged. Like Toffee, however, he forced a frozen smile through his tears and rubbed his stomach luxuriously. "Umm-umm," he managed to say. "It sure hits the spot."

"And leaves it in ruins," Toffee agreed. "They must cook this stuff up in old lye vats…"

"Keep drinking," Marc whispered urgently. "And look happy."

"Okay," Toffee said grimly. "I'll die with a smile on my face, but it'll be the lie of the century." She lifted the bottle gamely and drank. "Oh, boy!" she rasped through drawn lips, "this whiskey is the answer to a drunkard's prayer."

Marc drank dutifully in turn.

"You said it!" he announced, tears streaming from his eyes. "It's delicious!"

"I could go on drinking it forever," Toffee wheezed, taking another gulp and clutching her throat. "It's so smooth!"

"Makes you want more and more," Marc said, shaking his head to clear it after a third libation. "It gives you a real boost."

"Let's not carry it too far," Toffee whispered. "If I drink any more of this mange medicine I won't be able to hit the barn side of it broad."

"Broadside of a barn," Marc corrected her weakly. "But you're right. We'd better make the pitch while we're still conscious."

Toffee nodded and made a great show of registering happy inspiration. "Say," she cried, "you know who would just love this whiskey?"

"No," Marc replied like the second part in a minstrel skit. "Who"?

"George!" Toffee said. "You remember good old George?"

Marc nodded vigorously. "Wouldn't he be just crazy about whiskey like this?"

"He certainly would. Crazy mad, he'd be. Isn't it too bad he's not here?" Then Toffee brightened. "But perhaps he is! You never can tell about good old George."

"But when we were talking to him earlier he didn't answer."

"Perhaps he misunderstood something one of us said," Toffee suggested. "Maybe he didn't understand our type of humor and got offended. You know, like when I said I was going to gouge his eyes out? A harmless remark to most people, but perhaps not so to good old George."

"True," Marc said sagely. "George always was sensitive." He glanced around the room. "George?" he called. "If you're here, old man, how about having a drink with us? If we said anything to hurt your feelings we certainly didn't mean to!"

He paused to listen. There was a hesitant shuffling across the room.

"Well…" a voice said uneasily.

Marc and Toffee exchanged glances of triumph.

"You mustn't miss out on this, old man," Marc cajoled. "You really mustn't."

"And it will make such a nice friendly gesture," Toffee put in, "to show that you forgive us our thoughtless little jibes."

"Well," the voice returned, a shade less hesitant. "I am a little dry."

"Of course you are," Marc said jovially, "and we have the very thing to bring you comfort and contentment. Just step over here and I'll give you this whole bottle."

"No tricks?" George asked warily.

"George!" Toffee said, thoroughly scandalized, "how can you even entertain such a notion?"

"Just to show you," Marc said, "why don't you stay invisible? You're perfectly safe that way."

"Okay," George agreed. "Just hold out the bottle."

"Right-oh," Marc said and turned to Toffee. "Give it everything," he whispered. Toffee nodded.

AS Marc held out the bottle, Toffee sighted on the area in line with his hand, on the principle that George, being a duplicate of Marc, his head would be on the same level. The best strategy, she felt, was to concentrate on this area as swiftly and violently as possible. She held the bottle in readiness and when, a moment later, the bottle jogged in Marc's hand, she was prepared. She swung as hard as she could in a wide horizontal swipe. About half way, the bottle jarred to an abrupt stop and shattered, spewing liquid and glass in all directions. This was subsequently followed by a surprised moan and a heavy thudding sound in the vicinity of the floor.

"Got him!" Toffee cried jubilantly. "Smashed him right on the button!" She dropped the jagged neck of the bottle daintily to the floor.

"He's still invisible," Marc said worriedly. "I hope there'll be developments."

Developments came almost immediately, and they were well worth watching, though hardly the sight for sore eyes. Marc's calculations had been correct. Surprised, as it were, into unconsciousness, George had completely lost control of his ectoplasm. The trouble, though, was that instead of splashing out through his body all of apiece, it trickled out in fits and starts.

What appeared on the floor, under Marc's and Toffee's watchful eyes, was not George in total; but a sort of jigsaw George in which many of the vital pieces had been omitted. While one could be grateful for George's head, there was bound to be a pang of regret for the neck which had failed to appear.

An arm lay to the left, with only a finger or two to indicate that it had once blossomed a hand. Had there ever been an expression to the effect that half a torso was better than none, George had disproved it beyond measure; a torso, apparently severed from the collar bone to the mid-riff was so much worse than no torso at all as to be positively hair-raising. A random foot here, an errant kneecap there only garnished the over-all picture of hideous human butchery. With a shudder of revulsion, Toffee turned from the awful sight.

"Leave it to George," she said, "just leave it to that monster to be as revolting as possible."

"I don't suppose it's really his fault," Marc said fairly, "but I wish he were invisible again."

It was at this moment that the congressman and his henchman, having completed their discussion in the front of the warehouse, arrived at the door of the storeroom and fitted a key to the lock.

"Duck!" Toffee said. "Get behind those crates!"

"What about you?"

"I'm going to get my invention back. Besides they can't hurt me, and the important thing is to give you a chance to escape."

"Okay," Marc nodded and faded into the dimness behind the crates.

TOFFEE moved to the nearest stack of boxes, boosted herself atop them and leaned back in an attitude of relaxed languor. She watched from the corner of her eye as the door swung open and the congressman and the thug advanced into the room. She lifted her gaze dreamily to the ceiling and began to hum quietly to herself.

"There she is, boss," the thug said. "There's the dame, up there."

"My word!" Congressman Entwerp said. "Where did Pillsworth ever pick her up?"

"In a Turkish bath, I guess, before they passed out the towels."

Toffee turned slowly and observed the two with heavy disdain.

"Please be quiet," she drawled, "you're disturbing my meditations."

"Where's Pillsworth?" the thug asked.

Toffee shrugged. "Somewhere around, I suppose."

"Okay, sister," the thug growled, "cut out the jazz. Where is he?"

"You're sure you want to know?"

"We insist," Congressman Entwerp said.

"Then just step nearer," Toffee said with an airy wave, "and feast your eyes. You will find Mr. Pillsworth—more or less—on the floor, just to the right of these boxes. I'm sure you'll excuse him if he doesn't rise to greet you."

Warily, the two men edged closer. Then suddenly the thug, catching sight of George in his disconnected condition, stopped short. His mouth worked soundlessly, and his eyes rolled loosely in their sockets. The congressman, not yet aware of George, looked at him.

"What's the matter with you?" he asked shortly. "Why are you standing there making faces? Stop that and…!"

The tirade ended abruptly as the congressman's gaze fell to George. He lost his breath in a thin wheeze.

For a long moment the two men simply goggled, then slowly they turned away.

"You fool!" the congressman screamed. "I only told you to finish him off, not to hack him up into cutlets!"

"But I didn't!" the thug said shakenly. "He was all right when I locked him in here."

"Then, who…!"

Together, the two of them turned and regarded Toffee with incredulous eyes. Toffee returned their stares with innocent directness.

"Yes, gentlemen?" she murmured.

"Did you…?" the congressman began, then broke off with a shudder.

"Did I what?" Toffee asked demurely.

"What the congressman means," the thug said in a whisper, "is did you…do that?"

"Oh, that," Toffee said. She returned her gaze thoughtfully to the ceiling as though trying to remember. Finally she shook her head. "No," she said. "I'm certain that's not one of my jobs. Too messy."

The men gaped.

"Holy smoke!" the thug quavered. "What happened to him?"

"Who knows?" Toffee shrugged.

"Maybe he has some horrible disease. I figure it's his business."

"Good God!" the congressman breathed. "We've got to get him off our hands. We'll have to be careful, though. The hospital has the entire police force out looking for him. It's on the radio. If we were caught with him in that condition the party wouldn't like it."

"Nobody would like it," the thug said. "Shall we dump him in the river?"

THE congressman shook his head. "Too many patrolmen around. There must be..." His voice trailed off into thoughtful silence. Finally he nodded with decision. "We won't try to hide him. We'll deliver him to the police just as he is—in an automobile crash. The girl too."

"Huh?" the thug said. "How do you mean?"

"It's simple enough. Pillsworth looks like a crash victim, so why don't we just let him be one? Go get a sack or something to carry him out in." He turned and moved toward the door. "I'll have Hank fix up one of the cars."

"Good night, boss," the thug said plaintively, following after him, "you mean I've got to pick him up—with my hands!"

The moment they were gone, locking the door after them, Toffee jumped down from her perch and Marc appeared from the shadows.

"Do you know who that was?" Marc asked excitedly.

"The old bird with the sable hairdo?"

Marc nodded. "It's Congressman Entwerp. I should have known he was behind this mess. And that isn't all; those crates of cheap whiskey are just a front. Underneath there's enough bacteria culture to wipe out the whole country. These boys are planning mass murder!"

"Also individual murder," Toffee said.

"What?"

"They're going to arrange an auto crash. When the wreckage is sorted out George and I will be prominent amongst the demolished extras."

"Good grief!"

"It's nothing to worry about," Toffee said. "After all, they can't possibly kill me—or George either, for that matter. In the meantime you can contact the police and see that they're arrested. There's just one thing though; you're going to have to get the police without letting the police get you."

"Huh?"

"It seems the entire force is out scouring the city for you, and I get the impression that they're supposed to rush you along to the operating room without messing around with any conversation."

"Golly," Marc said. "How am I going to work it? Even if I get a chance to tell them about Entwerp, they'll just think I'm delirious."

"Be your own bait," Toffee suggested. "Entwerp will be busy murdering George and me. All you have to do is get the cops to chase you to the scene of the crime so they can catch him red-handed. I'll see to it that the door's left unlocked long enough for you to get out of here…" She stopped as the key sounded again in the lock. "Anyway, work it out as you go along, and I'll see you later…"

CHAPTER NINE

"WHAT took so long?" the congressman demanded. He was standing by the green sedan, holding the door open.

"It was the dame," the thug said breathlessly. "When I turned to lock up the storeroom, she let out a yip and took off. I had to chase her all over the joint before I caught her."

At his side, Toffee shook her head to get the hair out of her eyes. "I just wanted a little exercise to get up the circulation," she said.

"We certainly circulated," the thug agreed sourly. "All over the place."

"You didn't leave the storeroom open?" the congressman asked.

"I went back and locked it."

"I see you got Pillsworth in the car."

"Yeah," the thug said. "But he handled awful funny, like he was all strung together with invisible wire. I had a job spreadin' him out in the seat."

The congressman looked at him sharply. "You've probably been drinking that dummy whiskey again," he said. "Anyway, let's get going. The girl will have to drive."

"I don't know how to drive," Toffee said. "Besides, I haven't got a license."

"Never mind, sister," the thug said, "that's even better." He nudged her toward the door of the car, as the congressman moved off into the night. Toffee gazed inward at the dismembered George sprawled across the seat.

"Do I have to get in there with him?" she asked.

"The boss doesn't want you to be lonesome," the thug said.

"I'd rather be lonesome," Toffee said, but she got into the car anyway.

The thug closed the door after her and leaned through the window.

"Just so you'll know," he said, "I'd better explain. This car hasn't any brakes, and the steering is fixed. It's okay now, but after a few minutes it will break and the car will be out of control. We have it timed out with the curve at the end of the speedway, the one called Dead Man's Curve. By the time you reach that the wheel will be just about as much good to you as a set of knitting needles. In other words, you're going to drive due south with your foot to the floor and crack up on the curve. No one's missed that curve yet and lived."

"There's always a first time," Toffee said brightly.

"Don't count on it, sugar. And just to make sure you do what you're told, the congressman and me will be alongside in the congressman's car. I personally will be holding a rod aimed at your head, so don't get notions. Also, we want to be around to report the accident."

Toffee nodded approvingly. "It only seems the sort of thing any good citizen would do," she said.

The gunman stared at her. "Too bad a good looking dame like you has to be so wacky."

"We all have our little flaws," Toffee said chattily. "That's life."

"Aren't you even worried?"

Toffee shook her head. "I've always wanted to learn to drive," she said, smiling.

"Oh, my God!" the thug moaned. "Maybe it's best; you're sure to kill yourself sooner or later anyway."

"Of course," Toffee said, patting his hand. "I don't want you to blame yourself. Just consider you're doing a public service."

MEANWHILE, a lanky figure had emerged warily from the warehouse and was lurking, in a twitchy sort of way, in the dimness of the alley. Obscured in shadow, Marc had watched Toffee get into the green sedan, the thug instructing her in the art of driving. He glanced anxiously down the street, praying for a police car.

A small coupe, with a man and woman inside, pulled up to the curb at the end of the block, and the man got out and disappeared into the telegraph office on the corner. But that was all.

Marc jumped as he heard the green sedan start up. He turned to see a black limousine, driven by the congressman, pull up beside it. The thug crossed and got inside and a moment later the barrel of a gun caught light from the window. Time was seeping out.

Ducking from cover, Marc raced for the coupe and the waiting woman on the corner. Reaching it, he threw the door open and jumped inside. The woman, a faded blond, pressed back against the seat with a startled cry. Marc, however, was too relieved at finding the key in the ignition to notice.

He started the car, threw it into gear and set it in motion almost in a single action. The woman's reaction to this was a shrill, braying scream.

"Please," Marc said distractedly. "Don't." The woman screamed again. "Do you have to do that?" he asked annoyedly.

"I have to do something, don't I?" the woman enquired wretchedly. "I can't just sit here, can I?"

"I don't see why not," Marc said, peering down the street intently. "It doesn't help anything to scream like that."

"It helps me plenty," the woman retorted hotly. "When naked men come leaping into a lady's car and driving her off to God knows what, it gives her a great satisfaction to scream." As though to prove her point she paused to scream again. "Anyway, it makes her feel a hell of a lot better."

"I don't see why," Marc said with rising irritation.

"Well, put yourself in my place," the woman snapped. "What would you do if a naked man came leaping into your car?"

"Naked men don't leap into my car." Marc said self-righteously. "I wouldn't let them."

"Are you suggesting that I invite naked men to come leaping into my car?" the woman asked frigidly. "I'll have you know…"

"The way you carry on about it," Marc said, "one just automatically draws his own conclusions. One pictures a whole procession of naked men just waiting their turn to leap into your car, you're such an authority on these occasions."

FOR a moment the blond fell into a sulky silence. She glanced out the window at the rapidly passing scenery.

"What I want to know," she said at length, "is what is my husband going to say."

"Not knowing your husband," Marc said, "I'm in no position to guess. If I were you I'd judge by the way he's expressed himself on other similar occasions."

"There you go again," the woman said, "insulting me. Where are you taking me?"

"I'm not taking you anywhere," Marc said. "I'm taking myself. You just happened to be here."

"Oh," the woman said, not, it seemed, without a touch of disappointment. There was another lapse of silence.

"Do you know where there's a cop?" Marc asked, after a few more blocks.

"If I did," the woman said, "I'd be with him instead of you. What do you want with a cop?"

"I've got to find one," Marc said anxiously. "It means everything."

By this time the woman had resigned herself to the unhappy fact that she was out for a spin with a raving lunatic. She nodded sagely, as though agreeing with this last remark entirely.

"Sure," she said, "sometimes I feel that way myself. Cops are everything. It just sweeps over me all of a heap."

"What sweeps over you?" Marc asked absently.

"Cops," the woman said.

"Do you think you ought to be making these little confessions to a total stranger?" Marc asked distastefully. "Or do you mean your husband is a cop?"

"Of course not," the woman said. "My husband is a butcher. What's that got to do with it? I was just saying that sometimes cops just seem to surge over me." She giggled with nervous desperation. "A sort of blue serge, you might say."

"Well," Marc said, "since you seem to know all these cops so well, you ought to be able to tell me where they hang out."

"I don't know all these cops," the woman said.

"You mean they're a bunch of total strangers?" Marc asked, thoroughly shocked. "My word!"

"Couldn't we just drop the subject?" the woman asked defeatedly. "I'm all confused somehow."

"I should think you would be confused," Marc agreed. His voice trailed away on a rising inflection as he spotted a police car parked at the curb across the street. "Cops!" he breathed. He glanced ahead. "You see that green sedan up ahead with the black limousine beside it?"

The woman nodded vaguely.

"The one that just cut up over the sidewalk? What about it?"

"Keep your eye on it," Marc instructed, "while I get the cop's attention. It's a matter of life and death."

CHAPTER TEN

THE green sedan, as it turned out, was eminently worth keeping an eye on. Toffee, beleaguered as she was with the mechanics of keeping the vehicle in motion, had come upon other problems. Early in the game, feeling vague stirrings at her side, she had looked around to see George's dismembered head yawn thickly and open its eyes. Then, as if this wasn't loathsome enough, a set of fingers wriggled to the edge of the seat, gripped it and boosted the halved torso around so that the disjointed feet dropped to the floor. George, rising from unconsciousness had hauled himself into a sitting position. Toffee looked on this development without favor.

"Stay down, George," she hissed. "Get back where you were."

The head swiveled around hideously, a wounded look in its eyes.

"Oh, it's you, is it?" he said sadly. "You hit me."

"And I'll hit you again," Toffee promised, "if you don't get down."

George merely looked baffled at this. "Where are we goin'?" he asked.

"To an accident," Toffee said.

George's face brightened. "Was Marc in it?" he asked.

"It hasn't happened yet," Toffee explained. "We're going to be in it, you and I. In fact, we're the whole accident."

"Huh?" George said, edging up a bit. "Us?"

"That's right," Toffee nodded. "They figure we know too much."

"Too much about what?"

"About this subversive business," Toffee said. "They think we know their plan to overthrow the government."

"So they're going to kill us in an accident?"

"Uh-huh."

"Aren't you scared?"

Toffee shrugged. "Why should I be? I'm a product of Marc's mind. I can't possibly be destroyed unless he is. And he's perfectly safe."

"He is?" George said, his voice heavy with disappointment. "Why don't these people want to kill him?"

"They think they are killing him," Toffee said. "They think you're Marc. In fact they believe you're already dead."

"What!" George cried. "You mean I'm acting as a decoy to save Marc's life?"

Toffee nodded smugly. "Some onions, eh, George?"

"Stop the car!" George shouted. "Let me out!"

"No brakes," Toffee said. She nodded toward the limousine. "Besides, they won't let me. You'd better get down in the seat or they'll think it's funny."

"I hope they do," George said sullenly, "I hope they think it's funny as hell and do something about it. It's so damned unfair." And with that he leaned across Toffee, jutted his head out the window and began baying in the direction of the limousine.

"Stop that!" Toffee said. "It sounds awful."

GEORGE swiveled his frightful head around in her direction. "It should," he said. "It's the Torment Lament. I learned it in the Moaning Chorus and it's guaranteed to drive you mad in nothing flat." He turned back to the night and the limousine and sent his voice wailing into the wind.

It was an effort that was not lost on its audience. The occupants of the limousine looked around sharply with horrified eyes.

"Jesus in Heaven!" the thug gasped.

At his side the congressman was so taken with the fearsome recital that he completely forgot he was driving. As the car careened dangerously, the thug reached out and pulled the wheel.

"Isn't it awful, boss?" he breathed.

"Awful doesn't begin to tell it," the congressman choked. "It's—it's awful!"

"Yeah. That's what I mean to say."

"How can anything sound like that?" the congressman asked hauntedly.

"If it can look like that," the thug said, "I guess it shouldn't have no trouble soundin' like that."

"And look at that girl, will you? She's actually talking to the filthy thing."

"She looks plenty hot under the collar."

"Why not? I'd be sore as hell myself."

"When do we get to the curve, boss?"

"I don't know," the congressman said. "But I can't wait. The sooner that car crashes and takes that frightful thing with it the better."

CHAPTER ELEVEN

MEANWHILE, as the two cars skidded and reeled toward the appointed spot of disaster, Marc continued to loiter several blocks behind. Having deliberately cut across traffic in the middle of the block, he pulled up beside the police car and leaned out the window.

"I just cut across traffic!" he called out.

The cop behind the wheel left his conversation with his companion and observed Marc dubiously.

"So what?" he asked. "You want me to give you a gold star on your driver's license?"

"I don't have a driver's license," Marc offered hopefully. "What are you going to do about it, you big, thick-headed slob?"

The cop turned back to his partner. "A kidder, we've got here," he said. He turned back to Marc. "Beat it, comedian, you and your girl friend take off."

"Aren't you going to chase me?" Marc asked. "I'm a lawbreaker."

"Move along, chum," the cop drawled, "before I sell you a ticket to the orphan's picnic."

"But you've got to chase me," Marc said urgently.

"No I don't, friend," the cop said. "I've got to sit here and listen for radio leads on this goofy Pillsworth guy."

"But that's me!" Marc said. "I'm Pillsworth!"

The cop looked at him with forced patience. "Sure, sure," he said. "And I'm Miss Atlantic City. Beat it." He turned back to his companion.

"What if I told you I knew where a murder was going to happen?" Marc ventured.

The cop looked around. "You're just full of news, aren't you?" he said, and turned away again.

For a moment Marc sat in silent indecision. Then he turned to the blond.

"Why don't you scream?" he asked.

"Why should I?" the woman asked interestedly. "Do you really know where a murder's going to happen?"

"You said screaming made you feel good," Marc suggested.

"I feel fine," the woman said. "I always do with a lot of stuff going on. Who's going to get murdered?"

Marc glanced desperately from the woman to the cops and back again. A determined look came into his eyes. He cautiously extended two fingers to the woman's thigh. "I'm sorry," he said, and pinched as hard as he could.

THE results were everything to be wished for—and more. Stiffening in her seat, the woman let out a bleat that surpassed even her previous efforts. Even George might have envied the torment in her voice as it soared, swooped, scaled the heights and dipped into soul-shattering depths. At its completion, the blond turned and took a clawing swipe at Marc's face.

Marc ducked. "That's the stuff!" he said happily, noting from the corner of his eye that he had finally gained the undivided attention of the police force. Pinching the blonde again and nodding his satisfaction at the second chorus, he threw the coupe into gear, cut across traffic and headed down the speedway. It was only a moment before the wail of a siren mingled with the shrill vocalizations of his companion. He pushed the gas feed to the floor.

To the witnesses along the speedway, the pedestrians, the vendors, the shop owners and just plain malingerers, the events of the evening were never entirely clear. Some, judging simply by the volume of noise, settled for the notion that what had passed was nothing more than an overly exuberant wedding procession. The sticklers, however, rejected this notion flatly, pointing to the significant details of the affair.

Which, they demanded to know, was the wedding couple? Certainly it couldn't have been the redhead and the wailing man in the green sedan; certainly no bride—or at least very few—had ever used that kind of language to her groom on the wedding night. And it took the most wretched husband years to achieve the note of despair, which this poor fellow was loosing on the evening air.

As for the black limousine, that was out. Though its occupants seemed locked together in some sort of mad embrace, the arrangement appeared to have its roots in terror rather than affection.

The couple in the coupe that followed was even more difficult to wedge into the picture of the young couple united. After all, wasn't she screaming her lungs out and hammering on his head with both fists?

As for the police who followed and they probably knew the truth of the matter—they looked shocked to the core. So there simply wasn't any answer for it until the morning papers came out.

The participants in the demented chase along the speedway, however, were far too engrossed in their own problems to care for the conflict they introduced into the lives of innocent bystanders. Toffee, for one, could not have been less concerned; she was too mad at George.

"Stop that caterwauling!" she yelled. "Stop it, you idiot."

GEORGE pulled his disconnected head inside the window and eyed Toffee owlishly. His other parts adjusted themselves and the head sank into Toffee's lap. There, gazing up at her, it lazily crossed its eyes and began to whimper piteously.

"Ugh!" Toffee cried. "I'll go mad!"

The head relaxed its face obligingly into an expression of feebleminded delight, letting its tongue loll loosely from the corner of its mouth.

"That's all!" Toffee screamed. "I'm getting out of here!"

Without further consideration for the occupants of the limousine and the approaching curve, she relinquished the wheel, threw the car door open, and with one last agonized glance at the loathsome head, which was now foaming prettily at the mouth, prepared to depart its company. In the limousine this bit of action was not unobserved.

"She's trying to get away!" the congressman yelled. "Stop her!"

The thug turned to the window and looked. "Get back!" he hollered. "Get back or I'll blast you!"

"Go ahead," Toffee cried. "It'll be a positive pleasure next to what I've just been through."

"Okay!" the thug said grimly. "You asked for it!"

His finger closed down on the trigger. It was just at that moment, however, that the green sedan, no longer benefitted by a driver, swerved toward the limousine, throwing Toffee back inside. The congressman cramped the wheel of the limousine sharply to avoid a crash. The gunman, thrown sharply against the door, fired wildly into the night. From the rear there was the sound of screeching tires and forced brakes.

"Good night!" the congressman panted, righting the limousine as the green sedan veered away again. "What did you hit?"

"I think it was that coupe back there," the thug said, peering out the window. "I must have hit a tire; it's out of control."

"Good Lord!" the congressman yelled, "the curve's right ahead! We're pinned in between them. We're going to crash. Everybody's going to crash!"

No sooner was this dire prediction out of the congressman's mouth than it became a deafening reality. Ahead, the green sedan raced headlong into the concrete embankment with a rending smash and almost literally flattened itself into two dimensions.

This was the signal for the two lesser crashes that followed. The limousine engaged its radiator forcibly into the wreckage just in time to receive a skidding broadside from the coupe.

A MOMENT of silence followed, emphasized by the approaching scream of a siren. The police car jolted to a stop and the two cops ran forward to the scene of destruction. They reached the coupe first.

"Here!" the first cop said. "What's going on?"

The faded blonde jutted her head out of the window. "He blew out my tire!" she rasped. "Not to mention all that pinching!"

"Pinching?" the cop asked curiously. "What kind of pinching, lady? Where?"

"All kinds of pinching," the woman said evilly. "Everywhere."

The cop peered at Marc. "Why's he dressed in that nightshirt?"

"How should I know?" the woman said. "Maybe he thinks he's cute or something."

The cop leaned closer. "Here, you," he said, "why are you dressed like that?"

"I'm tired," Marc said exhaustedly, "and I want to go to bed. I had a little drink about an hour ago..."

"Stop that now," the cop barked. "No nonsense."

"But it's all perfectly true," Marc said.

The cop started to speak further, hut he caught sight of the congressman and his companion climbing out of the limousine and tore himself away.

"There are people dying in that car!" the congressman shouted tragically, hurrying forward. "It's awful, officer!"

"All maimed and cut up," the thug put in. "Loose heads and legs and stuff all over the place."

"Have you seen them?" the policeman asked.

"Well, they must be," the congressman put in quickly. "How could it be otherwise? The man in the car is Marc Pillsworth. I saw him just before the crash."

The policeman did a take. "Yeah?"

"Sure," the thug said excitedly. "Only now he's all cut up—loose head and arms and...!"

"Shut up," the congressman snapped.

"They might still be alive," the cop said. "We've got to do something about it."

"Indeed we do," the congressman said. "Perhaps we can assist them."

"Come on," the cop said. "You can give a hand."

DUTIFULLY the three turned to the sedan. They turned and then stopped with a harmonized gasp, the cop taking the bass. In the moment of their turning there had been a sudden movement in the car and the door had swung partially open. In the opening there appeared a leg of provocative shapeliness.

"A leg!" the thug shuddered. "I told you!"

"A dame's leg," the cop breathed. "And just think what the rest of her must have been like with a leg like that! Just imagine...!" He sucked in his breath as the leg began to show unexpected signs of life. It quivered, turned and was quickly joined by a mate of equal perfection. It was only a moment before Toffee appeared in total, quite unmarked. Her mood, however, was hostile. Quitting the ruined car she turned back to the door and thrust her head inside.

"Of all the beastly, rotten, evil-minded, stinking things to do to a girl!" she snapped. "Come out of there you slimy-souled son of Satan and fight like a man. I'll teach you to make foul passes at a girl when she is stuck under a clutch. I'll show you...!"

"Good gosh!" the cop said. "Who's she talking to?"

"She must be hysterical," the congressman said, thoroughly shaken. "Probably got a crack on the head and isn't accountable for what she's saying."

"That's certainly no way to talk to the dead," the cop said.

"It's no way to talk to the living," the thug said. "If she hauled off at me like that I'd rather be dead."

"The poor child's obviously insane," the congressman said firmly. "There's no question about it."

Meanwhile Toffee was still at it. "Come out of there, you hulking lout," she grated, "before I come in there and drag you out by your ears!"

"Poor little thing," the cop said sadly. "She really believes Mr. Pillsworth can come out of that car. She refuses to believe he's dead."

By now Toffee had stepped forward and yanked the door all the way open. As the three in the background stared in varying degrees of apprehension, a thin figure in a brief linen gown crawled out on its hand and knees. The congressman swayed slightly as though about to faint.

"You look more natural down on all fours, you beast," Toffee rasped. "I ought to kick you right in the slats. Get up and try to face me if you've the nerve!"

APPARENTLY the shock of the accident had given George's ectoplasm a further jolt for now he was completely materialized. He looked up at Toffee ruefully and got to his feet.

"I was only trying to get you loose," he said.

"The way you were pawing me was enough to get any girl loose," Toffee said. "Just don't try it again."

"Gawd a'mighty!" the thug whispered. "Pillsworth!"

"Pillsworth?" the cop said. "But that's the same guy who was pinching the other dame in the coupe. My gosh! how he gets around!"

Just then the other policeman, who had retreated to the background, arrived on the scene with Marc and the blond in custody.

"Hey," he said, "I caught this creep on the creep. He was trying to sneak out."

The cop looked quickly at Marc, then back to George. "It's the same guy!" he said. "Which one of you birds is Pillsworth?"

Marc and George went smoothly into their routine of pointing to each other in unison.

"He is!" they said.

The cop turned to Toffee. "Do you know which is which?" he asked.

"Sure," Toffee said and nodded at George. "He's Pillsworth."

"She's crazy," George retorted hotly. "She's as crazy as bedbugs in a bathtub."

"That's right," the thug put in. "She's a looney if there ever was one."

Marc moved urgently to gain the cop's attention. "You've got to arrest that man," he said, pointing at the congressman. "He's a subversive and a murderer."

THE congressman whirled about. "You must be insane, sir!" he rasped in frantic denial.

"You must be," Marc said. "You must have been ripe for the hatch years ago."

"You're a fine one to talk," the blonde put in nastily. "Officer this man is off his rocker like a busted hobby horse. He's done nothing but pinch me ever since we met."

Toffee levelled her gaze at Marc. "What were you doing pinching that tomato?" she demanded. "Just what were you getting at?"

"Oh, don't be crazy," Marc said distractedly.

"Oh, so I'm crazy, am I?" Toffee said, doubling her fists.

"You sure are, sister," the thug put in. "You're the most hopped up dame I ever saw." He turned to the cop. "She ought to be locked up."

"Oh, yeah?" Toffee said. "At least I didn't put anyone in a busted car and send them off to get killed. Officer, I want you to arrest that killer."

"Look, officer," Marc insisted, "you've got to take this man into custody. He's a menace to the whole country."

"If you take anyone in, officer," the blond put in harshly, "make it this skinny bimbo. Pinch him like he pinched me."

The congressman moved in aggressively toward Marc. "You're making slanderous accusations!" he blustered. "You should be committed to an institution!"

"You're crazy!" Marc raged.

"You're crazy!" the blond screeched.

"You're crazy!" Toffee hollered at the blond.

"You're crazy!" the thug insisted moodily.

The cop turned dizzily to his companion and held out a palsied hand. "Hurry!" he pleaded, "call the wagon, and let's take the whole bunch of them in. In another minute I'm going to be crazy!"

CHAPTER TWELVE

THE morning sun poured through the high windows of the courtroom, wasting its brightness on a scene of sullen dementia. Judge Carper's heavy face had achieved a shade of dyspeptic vermilion in record time this morning. Even the flies clung to the walls in muted terror as his gavel banged on the substantial wood of the bench and set the room atremble.

"Silence!" the judge roared. "Silence, damnit! And if one more defendant makes just one more crack about the sanity of any other defendant I'll lock the whole crew of you up and melt the key down for a watch fob." He ran his shaking hand over his forehead. "Besides, so far I don't even know which ones of you are the defendants and which are the complainants." He turned to the policeman. "Do you know?"

"I'm not sure," the cop admitted uneasily. "I think they're all both."

"Both what?" the judge asked confusedly.

"Both defendants and complainants. As far as I can tell everybody's mad as hell at everybody else. It sort of goes around in a circle."

"And I'm burned up at the lot of them," the judge said malignantly. "Who are those two over there without any clothes on?"

"I think they lost their clothes in the crash," the cop said vaguely. "The guy is really two guys, so it's hard to tell."

"What?"

"There are really two guys like that," the cop said. "Dressed alike."

The judge peered across at Marc with deep speculation. "I only see one of him," he said dryly.

NO TIME FOR TOFFEE

"The other one disappeared," the cop said, casting down his eyes. "He—well, sort of evaporated."

"Evaporated? What are you talking about?"

"It's a fact, your honor. It happened on the way in. The only way I can explain it is that one minute he was there and the next he just sort of melted away."

"Rooney," the judge said, "have you lost your wits?"

"It wouldn't surprise me, judge," the cop sighed. "Everyone else has. Why not me?"

"There's only one man there, Rooney," the judge said harshly. "And judging by those skinny legs of his, maybe not even that."

"Yes, sir."

"Are you bucking for another vacation, Rooney, is that it?"

"Well, your honor, I do feel tired. It seemed to come over me all of a sudden, after I ran into all those people."

"All right, we'll see what can be done. In the meantime let's have no more of this falderol about one man being two, only one of them evaporated."

"YES, your honor," Rooney said, greatly saddened. "There's only one man. I guess I was mistaken."

"Or drunk," the judge murmured sourly and turned his gaze to the assortment before him. "Now what happened with this gang?"

"They were all in a wreck that involved three cars. The young lady in the underskirt was driving the first one. She claims that the dark man with the scar tried to murder her by forcing her to drive a car with a broken steering gear."

"What does he say?"

"He says the young lady is mentally unstable and of low character. It seems that he and the congressman observed her in the car for some time before the crash. They say that

181

her behavior was most erratic, that she wailed and shrieked and at one point tried to abandon the car in full motion."

"How else can you abandon a car?" the judge said sharply. "You have to be in full motion."

"I mean the car was in full motion."

"I see. Where was this gentleman and the congressman while they were doing all this observing?"

"They were in the second car. The congressman was driving. The dark man is his bodyguard. He was cleaning his gun at the time and that's how he happened to shoot the third car, although the young lady insists he was trying to shoot her."

"I think I've lost the thread," the judge said foggily. "Who was in the third car?"

"The man with the skinny legs who says he isn't Pillsworth and a blond woman."

"He says he isn't Pillsworth and a blond woman?" the judge asked, his eyes loosening in their sockets. "Why should he say a thing like that?"

"No, no," the cop said earnestly, "he just says he isn't Pillsworth."

"Then he admits to being a blond woman?" the judge gasped. "He must he mad!"

"No," the cop said, "he doesn't admit anything about being a blond woman."

"Then he denies being a blond woman," the judge said with relief. "I wish you'd give me this story straight. Who accused him of being a blond woman in the first place?"

"No one," the cop said, almost tearfully. "He was only accused of being Pillsworth."

"Pillsworth? You mean the fellow the hospital's looking for? Who said he was Pillsworth?"

A look of doom came into the cop's eyes. "The—the other one, your honor," he said.

"The other what?" the judge glowered. "Stop being evasive and answer my questions."

ROONEY swallowed fatefully. "The other Pillsworth," he answered. "He accused Pillsworth of being Pillsworth—that is unless he's Pillsworth himself. Only he melted away so I guess we'll never really know. The blond woman insists she can't identify him."

There was a dreadful silence as the judge tapped the palm of his hand with the gavel. He lifted his gaze to the ceiling then leveled it slowly on Rooney.

"So we're back to the blond woman again, are we?"

"I'm afraid so," Rooney admitted weakly. "That's her over there, looking mad."

"I had hoped we were through with the blond woman," the judge said acidly. "I thought we'd washed the blond woman up."

"No, your honor, I'm afraid not."

"This isn't the same blond woman that Pillsworth denies being is it?"

"No, sir."

"Does she deny that she's Pillsworth, is that it?"

"No, sir," Rooney sighed hopelessly. "She's just a blond woman. She refuses to give her name because her husband's a butcher."

"Is she a defendant or a complainant?"

"A complainant," the cop said. "She said that Pillsworth stole her car and pinched her. That is if he's Pillsworth, and he denies it."

"Don't you mean he pinched her car?"

"No, sir. He stole her car, but he pinched her—on the thigh."

"My word!" the judge said.

The cop nodded. "She wants to sue someone, only since there were two of them she doesn't know which one did the pinching. She can't be sure whether it was this Pillsworth or the other one—if you follow my meaning."

The judge paled. "Are you being deliberately cryptic, Rooney, or is it simply that you can't see your way clear to be clear, if I make myself clear."

"I'm afraid I don't follow you, your honor."

"Just a taste of your own medicine, Rooney," the judge said vengefully. "How do you like it?" He turned his gaze moodily on the blond. "About this blond…?"

"Yes, your honor?"

"She gets everything all snarled up. Every time she enters the picture it ceases to make sense. Do you suppose this would all clear up if I just had her thrown out of court?"

"I don't think so. With or without her, things are snarled up just the same. I've never seen so much snarling in all my life; these people just don't seem to like each other."

"What about this fellow who denies he's Pillsworth?" the judge asked. "Is he the only pure defendant in the bunch?"

"Oh, no, your honor. He's the biggest complainant of the lot. And he's far from pure. He's accusing the congressman of being the head of a gang of subversives who are planning to kill the entire population with bacteria."

THE judge leaned across the bench, plainly scandalized. "The congressman!" he gasped. "Why Congressman Entwerp was a classmate of mine!"

"Yes, your honor. And he's threatened suit against this fellow for slander."

"Good," the judge said. "Have this Pillsworth or whoever he is brought before the bench. Obviously, he's a low criminal type. It sticks out all over him."

The cop nodded and turned in Marc's direction. "You," he said. "The judge will hear you."

Across the room, however, Marc gave no sign of hearing. Instead, he was gazing intently at the vacant chair next to his own. On his face was an expression of anxious annoyance.

"Now, look, George," he said, "You owe it to humanity to show yourself and help get this mess cleared up. Why not be a good loser for a change?"

The empty chair shifted, just perceptibly, with an air of complacency.

"Maybe they'll hang you," George replied hopefully from thin air.

"Don't be silly," Marc said. "There's no reason why they should. Come on, now; be a good fellow and help get this over with."

"Oh, I'm going to help get it over with," George said pleasantly. "When I'm through, they'll lower the boom on you so hard you'll be the first man in history to be buried in an envelope."

Just then Toffee leaned forward and touched Marc's arm. "The judge wants to speak to you," she said. "Come on, let's go!"

Marc glanced around. "Did he call you too?"

"Well, no," Toffee admitted, "but I'm an interested party. I want to see that you get fair treatment."

"Couldn't you just stay out of it?" Marc pleaded. "Couldn't I just handle this myself?"

"Nonsense," Toffee said. "You need me. Come on, the old gaffer's beginning to look apoplectic again."

"Oh, all right," Marc sighed. Getting up he followed Toffee to a position before the bench. The judge glowered down at them critically.

"So glad you finally found you could come," he said.

"Thank you," Toffee beamed. "It's nice of you to have us."

The gavel barked irritably. There was silence until the judge's eyebrows ceased to twitch.

"What are you doing here?" the judge enquired with forced composure. "Who called you forward?"

"Lots of people have called me forward," Toffee said, "but that's just talk, judge. I'm just impulsive."

"Silence!" the judge said. "Good God, girl, no one asked you for any sordid confessions. I just want to know what you're doing here?"

Toffee nodded toward Marc. "I'm with him," she said.

"Then he's the man who was with you in the green sedan?"

"Oh, no." Toffee shook her head. "He's the other one."

The judge blanched. "The other one?" he asked apprehensively.

Toffee nodded. "They're exactly alike. Only this one is nicer. That's why I switched."

The judge raised his gavel warningly, and turned to Marc. "Are you twins, sir?"

Marc opened his mouth to speak, but before he could George's voice sounded immediately behind him.

"Do I look like twins, you thick-headed joker?" the voice asked. "And if you must drink in the morning, for Godsake layoff the cheap stuff so you don't see double. I always heard justice was blind but I didn't know it was blind drunk."

THERE was an ominous silence in the court as the judge raked Marc with a glance of pure loathing. "Are you deliberately in contempt of court?" he asked.

Again Marc started to speak and again the voice beat him to it. "In it?" it said. "I'm fairly swimming in high octane contempt."

The blond who had been watching these proceedings with growing agitation suddenly sprang from her chair. "That's him!" she yelled hysterically. "I'm positive!"

"Be quiet, you!" the judge barked. "I've had enough out of you!"

"But he pinched me!" the blond cried.

"You're lucky that's all he did," the judge snapped.

"But you don't know where!"

The judge eyed her distantly. "With that lumpy figure of yours," he said, "it could scarcely matter. Now, shut up." He turned back to Marc. "I understand you've been making libelous remarks against Congressman Entwerp."

Marc looked around hopelessly, afraid to open his mouth lest George would take over again. He compressed his lips into a thin line.

"Speak up, man!"

Marc looked up unhappily. "I—I—" he murmured fearfully.

"What's the matter with you?" the judge asked. "Let's hear your accusations against my good friend the congressman."

"The congressman?" Marc ventured, then brightened as he noticed there was no interference from George. "Oh, yes. The congressman must be imprisoned at once, your honor. He's a national menace. He instigated a propaganda program to dope the public against the threat of the foreign powers. But worst of all, he has enough bacteria culture to murder the entire population."

"And what's more," Toffee broke in, "he pinched my gadget."

The judge's eyes swiveled about hauntedly. "He what?"

"Pinched my gadget," Toffee insisted. "The one with the button."

"Now just a minute," the judge said a little wildly. "Wasn't it the blond woman who had her gadget pinched?"

"Don't be silly," Toffee said. "She hasn't a gadget to be pinched."

"She hasn't?" the judge said in a startled whisper. "What happened to her gadget?"

"I guess she just didn't have one in the first place," Toffee said. "You can't just go out and buy them, you know."

THE judge turned to the cop. "Do you know anything about why this blond woman doesn't have a gadget?" he asked interestedly.

"Search me," the cop said. "I didn't know she didn't. Maybe it's because her husband's a butcher. Maybe…"

"Don't," the judge cried, shuddering. "Don't go on! I don't even want to think about it."

"Well, who cares about her gadget anyway?" Toffee asked bewilderedly. "It's my gadget I'm trying to tell you about."

"And I don't want to hear about it," the judge said shortly. "This court is no place for examination room discussions."

"Or much of anything else," Toffee retorted angrily. "Especially justice."

"Look, judge," Marc put in desperately. "You've got to listen to me. About all this bacteria…"

"Bacteria?" the judge said, startled. "What about bacteria?"

"It's a threat," Marc said. "It's got to be stopped."

The judge nodded. "My dentist said the same thing the other day. Are you a dentist?"

"Of course I'm not a dentist," Marc said. "It's the congressman."

"That's preposterous," the judge said. "The congressman isn't a dentist, never has been. You're just trying to rattle me."

Again, as Marc started to speak, the voice from behind took over. "That's rich, that is," it slurred. "You were rattled the day you were born, you old tosspot, and you've been getting balmier ever since. If you have the brain of a gnat..."

The gavel smashed down on the bench like the crack of doom.

"Go!" the judge said. "Go and leave me alone! You're all trying to drive me out of my mind."

"With a mind like yours," Toffee said, "it would be a fast drive on a kiddy car."

"Go!" the judge screamed. "Go away!"

Defeated by sheer volume, Marc and Toffee retreated back to their chairs and sat down. The one next to Marc's scraped back a trifle of its own volition.

"You fiend!" Marc hissed at the empty chair. "That was a fine mess, wasn't it?"

"Glad you admire my work," George said complacently out of thin air. "Isn't it remarkable how exactly alike our voices sound?"

"Go to hell," Marc said sullenly.

"If I do I'll probably meet you there," George said. "The old boy has you marked down for a sanity test. I heard him say so as you left up there. Somehow it warms me to think of you locked up with a bunch of homicidal maniacs. Who's to say what might happen to you?"

The gavel rapped on the bench again, this time more calmly.

"I'd like to speak to the congressman," the judge announced. "Not that I put any stock in the ridiculous accusations of that black-hearted nit-wit, but I would like to talk to someone rational for a change."

Across the room, the congressman rose from his chair with portly composure.

"I'm happy for the opportunity to defend myself against the ravings of this lunatic," he said smoothly, "though I'm certain the court hasn't taken them the least bit seriously."

"Of course not, congressman," the judge said grandly. "This court is always fair and impartial. Step up and have a chair. I'm sorry I can't offer you a drink during session, but perhaps we could have lunch together somewhere?"

"Good grief!" Toffee whispered. "They're carrying on like old sweethearts."

THE congressman smiled pityingly at Marc. "Actually, I have the greatest compassion for our poor friend here," he said magnanimously. "Who knows what dreadful experience drove him out of his senses?"

"Why the old foghorn!" Marc hissed between clenched teeth. "He's got enough gall to float a fleet."

"As for his fantastic charges," the congressman continued, "they're almost too silly to refute." He beamed on the judge. "I think you know just about how subversive I am, your honor."

The judge smiled broadly. "Call me Ralph," he said.

"Okay, Ralph," the congressman smiled. "And about that bacteria business; the only bacteria culture I have is home in the refrigerator. I just happened to let some cheese go moldy."

The judge laughed immoderately. "Oh, Congressman!" he gasped, wiping his eyes. "You always were a wit!"

Toffee frowned her disapproval. "This is worse than television," she said.

"What am I going to do?" Marc said. "I can't let him get away with it. I'll wind up in an asylum while he sells the whole country down the river."

Toffee nodded morosely. "We've got to think of something," she said. "If they won't listen to sense, I guess the only thing to do is resort to madness."

"How do you mean?"

"Trade seats with me," Toffee said. "I want to talk to George."

"It won't do any good. He won't listen to sense any more than the rest of them."

"That's all right," Toffee said. "What I have in mind is more nonsense—and a little hypnotism."

"Hypnotism?"

"Uh-huh. I told you I've been studying. Come on, trade."

AS unobtrusively as possible they changed seats. Toffee settled herself, crossed her legs with care, and turned to the vacant seat at her side. When she spoke her voice was husky and confidential.

"Look, George," she said, "I've been thinking..."

The chair quivered interestedly. "Yes?" George's voice said out of emptiness. "What about?"

"You and me," Toffee said. "I've just been going over things in my mind, and you know, George, I've really been sort of foolish."

"How do you mean?"

"Well take the way I always favor Marc against you. Suddenly it just occurred to me that there's no logical reason for it. After all you're just alike—except for a few little differences, of course."

"Oh?" George said, a note of interest creeping into his voice. "What differences?"

"Well, for instance, you're more aggressive, George. You have a more active, dynamic personality. You're the sort who knows what he wants and goes out after it."

"I suppose you could say that," George admitted. "What else?"

"You're cleverer, too. Look at the way you've got Marc bottled up right now, for example. He's a dead duck. In fact, to tell you the truth, George, you make Marc look pretty sick. I'm beginning to think a girl would be much better off with you."

George cleared his throat. "You're sure you mean it?" he asked.

"Of course I do," Toffee said. "Why wouldn't I, George? It's not just that you're cleverer and more dominant than Marc, there are other little things too, things only a woman would notice. Your eyes, for instance."

"My eyes?"

Toffee nodded. "Uh-huh. Your eyes are ever so much more exciting than Marc's. I don't know what it is, but there's a subtle difference. I guess it's personality. I've always noticed it."

"Oh, my eyes aren't all that good," George demurred. "Pleasant and friendly, perhaps, but..."

"Oh, much more than that," Toffee insisted. "Flashing and roguish."

"You really think so?"

"Certainly. That and more." Toffee paused for a moment, appeared hesitant. "George...?"

"Yes, Toffee?"

"Would you show me your eyes? Just materialize them for a moment so I can gaze into them?"

"Do you really like them that much?"

"Please, George..."

"Well...all right."

CHAPTER THIRTEEN

AND so it was that the congressman, long distracted by a view of Toffee fawning on a vacant chair, suddenly found himself staring across the room at two disembodied eyes which lolled in mid-air, swiveling and rolling about in a delirious attempt to be flashing and roguish. He coughed in a strangled way and glanced around at the judge.

The judge, had the congressman been astute enough to notice, had suddenly gone white about the gills and showed a shifty disinclination to meet his gaze. The truth of the matter was that the judge, similarly baffled by Toffee's seductive attitude toward the chair, had also been subjected to the nasty sight of George's grotesque eye exercises. He, like the congressman, had experienced a feeling of giddiness at the nape of the neck and decided against mentioning the incident. After gazing upon a pair of air-borne eyes, which have just crossed themselves in their zeal to convey the charm of the rake, one is generally loath to bring the subject up with anyone save the local psychiatrist. However, had either gentleman had the least inkling of the mad delights yet to come, they might have well bolted the room, shouting the news to the world.

The fact was that Toffee, in her endeavor to hypnotize George, was meeting with extraordinary success. Having gazed into George's eyes with his full cooperation it was only the matter of a moment before the hapless shade was completely mesmerized. The eyes, under Toffee's steady gaze, grew heavy, drooped, closed altogether, then reopened with a slightly dazed appearance. It was not a pleasant sight, but Toffee appeared to find satisfaction in it.

Not so, however, the judge and the congressman. Watching these developments with sidelong anxiety, they were sore put to it to continue with the business at hand.

"Yes, yes," the judge said vaguely, "you were telling me about this blackguard who's been saying all these filthy things about you…?"

"Eh?" the congressman said, starting. "Oh! Oh, yes. This fellow, the blackguard. I was saying that if he was half a man…!"

The congressman got no further for it was precisely in this moment that Toffee commanded George to materialize. There must have been, however, a lack of authority in her tone, for the results fell short of perfection. In fact, they fell short by exactly fifty percent. George, starting at the top of his head, blossomed rapidly into being down to the waist and there, quite devoid of his lower quarters, stopped. In effect, no sooner did the congressman speak of half a man than the order was filled to exact specifications. The congressman not only stopped speaking, but stopped breathing as well.

A NERVOUS hush fell over the courtroom, for by now several others had begun to notice the half portion George and were just as reticent to mention the matter as either the congressman or the judge. The judge clutched grimly to the bench for support and forced himself to look away. He laughed a dry, cackling laugh.

"Well, well," he said with feeble heartiness, "we mustn't fall into a reverie, must we? You haven't half—I mean you haven't really begun to tell me about these slurs against you, congressman."

There was something markedly distraught in the congressman's expression as he turned back to the bench. He fiddled with his tie, reached into his pocket, took something out and began to finger it nervously. It was Toffee's gadget.

"Well," he babbled. "I was only saying that anyone with half—I mean any mind at all would be able to see…uh…see…"

As he spoke, the congressman turned the gadget absently in his hand. It was on the fifth turn, when it was pointing directly at the judge, that his finger inadvertently snagged against the button and shoved it to one side. Instantly, as though the judge had never been there at all, the bench was starkly and dramatically deserted, with only the gavel left to mark its recent occupancy. The congressman gaped unbelievingly, shook his head, closed his eyes, then opened them again. The judge was still absent.

The congressman turned to the others and found himself and the bench the focal points for a sea of shocked eyes. He shuddered, pressed the gadget self-consciously in a fit of nerves. The button snapped in the opposite direction. In the next instant there was a shrill scream from the faded blond.

Those in court turned in unison to find that the judge, just as suddenly as he had departed, had reappeared. This time, however, he was comfortably ensconced in the lap of the distraught blond. In a courtroom where many odd things had recently taken place, it was the general consensus that when the judge of that court sneaks from the bench, creeps up on the nearest blond and hurls himself into her lap, some sort of climax has been reached. A murmur of indignation rose through the room.

The blond, for her part, agreed with the consensus, but did not stop at an indignant protest. Doubling up her fist she belted the judge a nasty blow in the eye.

"You mangy old goat!" she shrieked.

The congressman, by now in a veritable frenzy of nervousness, pressed the button again. This time it was

Toffee who disappeared. The murmur in the court became still more disturbed. The congressman twiddled the button in the opposite direction.

Miraculously, Toffee appeared behind the bench in the judge's position. She picked up the gavel and banged for attention.

"The court will come to order!" she shrilled happily. "Knock it off, everybody!"

A NEW kind of hush fell over the room. The congressman, slack-mouthed, looked up at Toffee with the fearful look of a man who has finally been backed to the wall on the question of his own sanity. The judge, nursing a blow on the left ear as another was being addressed to the right, looked up in horror.

"Here!" he yelled. "Get off that bench!"

"Get off that blond!" Toffee shot back. "You ought to be ashamed of yourself." She whirled about on the trembling congressman. "As for you, you big fat traitor, I want a clean confession and no nonsense."

"I don't have to talk to you," the congressman said uncertainly. "You can't make me say anything."

"Maybe not," Toffee said, "but what about your conscience?"

"Conscience?" the congressman said uncertainly.

"The term is unfamiliar to you?" Toffee said. "I'm not surprised. Let me try to explain it to you. A guilty conscience can play awful tricks on people." She eyed the congressman closely. "It can even make you think you're seeing things, for instance."

The congressman's eyes widened with an awful fear. "See—see things?" he quavered. "What kind of things do you mean?"

"Well," Toffee said reflectively, "say a man is responsible for another man's murder. If his conscience gets a hold of him he may begin to see that man as still alive. He may even see two such men, just alike. In really bad cases the subject is likely to imagine one of the men in a state of mutilation, say cut in half. Of course, that's pretty extreme."

The congressman glanced compulsively in George's direction and turned ashen. George, still at half-mast, stared back at him with fixed blankness. The congressman groaned.

"Then there's the very worst sort of conscience," Toffee went on. "That's when everything gets mixed up. Through a close study of recorded cases, we find that the first attack commonly occurs when the criminal is confronted with his crimes, usually publicly, as in a court of law."

"H-how do you mean?" the congressman whispered. "Whu—what happens?"

"Well, everything begins to appear to be just the opposite of what it really is. There is a famous English case in which the victim was so far gone that he actually believed that the magistrate on the bench had become a beautiful girl. He described the illusion, I believe, as a gorgeous redhead with an exquisite figure and legs too perfect to be true." Toffee laughed gaily. "Can you imagine anyone getting themselves looped up to that extent?"

The congressman forced a laugh that had all the light-hearted spontaneity of a coffin lid being pried up at midnight. "That boy was really gone, wasn't he—your honor?"

"Call me Ralph, old man," Toffee said.

"Of course, Ralph, old boy," the congressman said, blinking.

EXPERIMENTALLY, Toffee opened a drawer under the bench and withdrew a large black cigar. Inserting this into her month, she leaned forward toward the congressman. "Gotta light, friend?" she enquired.

The congressman started back sharply at this new incongruity. It was a moment before he recovered.

"Sure," he said, taking out a lighter and waggling it beneath the cigar. "Sure thing."

Taking a healthy puff on the cigar, Toffee leaned back luxuriously and blew out a cloud of smoke. "What say we adjourn?" she suggested. "We can slip around to the club and cut up a few touches with the boys."

"Well, all right," the congressman said, attempting a wan smile. "But…"

Toffee took the cigar from her mouth and leaned forward. "Yes, old man?"

"About these cases," the congressman said. "That fellow in England…"

"Oh, the one who thought the magistrate was a beautiful girl? It's hard to believe, of course, but you must remember it was an extreme case. The most severe ever recorded, I believe. The funeral was only a formality, of course, since there wasn't even a scrap of him recovered. Exploded, you know."

"Exploded!"

"That's right. The only thing of its kind in medical history. Poor devil went right off. With a great whopping roar, they said. The doctors said it was caused by repressed emotion."

"Oh, Mona!" the congressman groaned.

"Didn't mean to upset you, old friend," Toffee said. "It's an unpleasant thing to talk about."

"But couldn't they have saved him?" the congressman asked. "Suppose they had gotten him to a psychiatrist or something before it happened?"

"Actually it was much simpler than that," Toffee said ponderously. "The fellow could have saved himself merely by confessing. Confession, you know, is the only thing for a bad conscience. Highly recommended by all the best authorities. Those church people are doing it all the time—can't stop church people from confessing—and you never heard of one of them exploding, did you?"

"That's right," the congressman said hopefully. His gaze travelled out the window, a clouded look of inner turmoil on his face.

"It was just one of those things," Toffee put in. "One minute this chap was standing there in court just as hail and hearty as beans and the next—boom!—and the spectators were whisking him off their coat sleeves and passing round the cleaning fluid!"

The congressman whirled about in a convulsion of anguish. "I confess!" he blurted. "I confess everything!"

"Not everything," Toffee said. "Leave the racy personal stuff for another time."

The congressman reached out the gadget and dropped it on the bench. Toffee picked it up as he followed that contribution with a key.

"There's the key to the storeroom," the congressman said, "and the one to the private files. And here's a list of the members of the organization." He started as Rooney stepped forward and took him by the arm.

"Take him away," Toffee said blithely. "Find him a cell with lots of padding. And take his bodyguard too."

199

CHAPTER FOURTEEN

AS the congressman and the thug disappeared in the custody of Rooney, Toffee mashed out her cigar, quitted the bench and proceeded across the court where the blond was still throttling the judge.

"Better let him up, honey," she advised gently. "He's turning a very nasty blue."

The blond stopped to consider the judge's complexion and let him drop to the floor.

"Loathsome old bore!" she hissed as he sat up and rubbed his neck, then got to his feet and tottered off toward the bench. "That'll teach you next time."

Toffee moved on to Marc. "Well, don't just sit there," she said. "Let's get at it."

Marc looked up apprehensively. "At what?" he asked.

"Everything," Toffee said spaciously. "On the town."

"Haven't you had enough excitement?" Marc asked wearily.

"Not of the right sort," Toffee said. "What I crave is soft lights and wine and all that sort of elegant truck. Come on."

"What about George?"

"Oh, yes," Toffee reflected, "there is George, isn't there?" She regarded the transfixed half-spirit thoughtfully. "It would serve him right if we just left him here, cut off at the pockets. Still I don't suppose it's the thing to do." A look of inspiration came to her face. "I know."

Taking her gadget from beneath her arm, she leveled it at George and pressed the button. Instantly George disappeared entirely. Toffee replaced the instrument and turned to Marc.

"There," she said brightly. "George in the handy pocket size, where he can't do any harm. Now we're all set for a life of gin and sin and no interruptions."

"Now, wait a minute!" Marc said. "We're not set for anything, much less a life of gin and sin as you so pungently put it. Do I have to remind you that I have a wife to think of?"

"I don't care if you have a whole regiment of wives to think of," Toffee said testily. "I've protected and preserved you and, by gum, you're mine. At least right now. Your wife can just take her chances on what's left."

"If you continue with this scandalous talk," Marc said, shocked into primness, "I'm going to be forced to get up and walk right out of here."

"You take one step without me," Toffee warned, "and I'll break both your legs."

"Oh, well…" Marc sighed.

"That's better," Toffee nodded. "Of course I'll need some clothes, something terribly expensive and revealing…"

SHE broke off as the doors of the courtroom burst open and Julie, followed by the three doctors from the hospital, charged down the aisle.

"My God!" Marc cried. "Julie!" He swung around to Toffee. "Go away! Vanish!"

"I'm darned if I will," Toffee said. "I've stuck by you through all the thin and now I want some of the thick of it."

"Don't worry," Marc said miserably. "Just wait till Julie sees us; things will get thick in a hurry."

Even as Marc spoke the atmosphere began to congeal swiftly. Julie, having caught sight of the curious tableau formed by Marc and the scantily clad Toffee, jarred to a stop, digging her heels into the floor. A sharp, enraged sound came from her lips.

Julie, after her experience of the night before had recovered her physical faculties, but her emotional condition was still skittish. A wife, summoned to identify her dying husband, rather sets her mind on a scene of tearful sighs and murmured remembrances, with perhaps a touch of violin music in the background. When she finds her waning spouse looking perfectly alive and perky and in close proximity to a dangerous looking redhead, her bubble has a tendency to burst with a considerable bang.

"Marc Pillsworth!" Julie screamed. "Who is that woman!" And raising her handbag aloft she proceeded forward with mayhem unmistakably number one on her agenda.

Groaning, Marc rose from his chair. "She's going to kill me!"

Meanwhile, the doctors had also caught sight of Marc.

"There he is!" the first doctor said. "We'd better close in on him fast."

"It's amazing," the second doctor mused. "The man must be living sheerly on the energy of hysteria. He should have been dead hours ago." He turned to the third doctor. "Do you have the chloroform ready?"

The doctor nodded and exhibited a can and, a large sponge. "Wait till the Medical Association hears about this," he said excitedly. "They'll never believe it!"

Thus armed, the men in white pressed forward close in the wake of Julie.

Marc retreated in confusion toward the bench. "They're all after me!" he cried. "I can't stand much more of this. If just one more character tries to kill me...!"

THE doors of the court swung open and a tall, grim-lipped man barged into the room and down the aisle. He was carrying a large meat axe. Across the room the blond leaped joyously from her chair.

"Darling!" she yelled and ran to meet him. They came together in a tight clinch just inside the gate. "How did you find me, honey?"

"Bureau of Missing Persons," the man said cryptically. "Where is he?"

"Who, sweet?"

"This creep who kidnapped you. Point him out."

The blond glanced around. "That's him," she said, pointing, "the one with all those people following him."

The man observed Marc's retreating figure with a professional eye. "Not much meat on him," he judged, "especially around the shank." He shoved the blond aside. "This'll only take a second."

"Mother in heaven!" Toffee cried, "the whole population is out to get you." She pulled Marc out of reach of Julie's bag as it made a broad swipe at his head. "Come on, let's join the judge!"

Together, they raced around the bench and started to mount to the chair.

"Get away!" the judge screamed, taking in the ranks of Marc's attackers. "Don't come up here!"

"Sorry," Toffee said, leaping lightly up beside him and snatching up the gavel. "This is total war!"

Marc gaining the bench, turned his attention to Julie. "Please, dear!" he cried. "There's nothing to he sore about!"

"Oh, isn't there?" Julie gritted. "What about that naked little trull you're with?" She hefted the bag anew.

"Let me at him!" the enraged butcher bellowed from the flank. "I'll get him if I have to hack that bench away around him!"

In answer, Toffee brandished the gavel in a wide gesture of defiance, which terminated solidly on the side of the judge's nose.

"Ouch!" the judge roared, grabbing his face with both hands. "Clear the court!"

"Hell!" the butcher yelled. "I'm going to smear the court with that lousy kidnapper!"

The siege of the bench raged, and it will always be a sterling testimony to Julie's physical prowess that as she scaled the bench, the lethal handbag never once ceased to twirl over her head; if it happened to strike the judge more often than anyone else it was only because her aim was deflected by her overwrought emotions. To Marc and Toffee, however, the real menace lay in the butcher and his cleaver. Only by the most adroit maneuverings with the gavel was Toffee able to delay his murderous progress with a few strategic licks on the shins.

THE doctors, on the other hand, gave themselves over more to calculated strategy. While two of them tried to close in on Marc from the sides, the chloroformist, can and sponge held ready, crept up from the rear. They might have succeeded in this maneuver except for Toffee. The redhead, seeing that time and speed were of the essence, abandoned her attack on the butcher and sailed forward, the gavel raised in one hand, the gadget in the other. Her plan was to dispatch the flankers with a single action, then sweep on to overcome the third doctor with all dispatch. The strategy, however, was too hastily conceived to be really successful.

Marc in an effort to avoid Julie's bag, leaped forward at just the wrong moment. Throwing himself toward Toffee, he received the full impact of both the gavel and the gadget, one to the ear. He reeled to one side, stumbled and sprawled to the floor, shaking his head.

"Oh, no!" he wailed, looking back reproachfully at Toffee. "Not you too!"

But Toffee didn't answer; she was far too surprised and pleased at the sudden results of this little accident. In banging Marc over the head with the gadget, she had inadvertently sprung the switch and introduced George, completely restored to the last molecule, into the very center of the proceedings. She only regretted she hadn't thought of it sooner as she saw the attackers, in the confusion, turn on George in force.

"Stay down," she hissed and dropped down lightly beside Marc. "While George is standing in for you, let's get out of this."

Marc rose to his knees, took in the new development and nodded. "This way," he said, indicating a door behind the bench. "I saw the judge crawling out this way a minute ago."

Together they scuttled on their hands and knees to the door. Marc edged it open, let Toffee through, then followed after. Safe, they turned back to see how the battle was developing around the bench.

George appeared to be finding himself at rather a rude disadvantage. And it is entirely conceivable that the besieged spook might well have been confused in that his last conscious moment had been the one of promised amour just before Toffee hypnotized him. Now, suddenly restored to awareness, instead of a fawning redhead, he found himself confronted by what appeared to be a select group of the worst fiends of hell.

George's gaze grew more and more terrified as he took in the swinging handbag, the slashing meat axe and the intense, determined faces of the doctors. With a single shriek of despair, as the meat axe made a swipe at his ear, he staggered backwards and vanished into thin air.

"Poor George," Toffee giggled. "I've got a feeling he checked out for good just then. He looked like a ghost who's just remembered a previous engagement."

MARC got up, closed the door and flicked the latch. He stopped, glanced around at the room. It was some sort of inner chamber, resplendent of leather and polished wood, a place of durability and hard surfaces, lighted by a large brass lamp standing on an enormous oak desk. At the far end of the room a door stood ajar, opening onto a hallway which pointed the direction of the judge's recent escape. Marc crossed to it and closed and locked it.

"Well," Toffee said, perching herself lightly on the corner of the desk. "This is more like it. Private."

Marc turned wearily from the door. "Just leave me alone," he sighed. "Just let me sit down somewhere and relax. This is the first time in almost twenty-four hours that I haven't had someone at my heels trying to kill me."

"Poor Marc," Toffee said. "You do need a rest."

Marc started across the room toward a large leather-covered chair. He was nearly there when he caught his foot in the lamp cord and fell.

Even as he struck the floor he was aware of the crazy seesaw flashes of light traveling up and down the wall. It wasn't until he rolled over, however, that he saw the lamp teetering precariously on the edge of the desk just above his head. He started to cry out, but before he could force the sound to his lips the lamp slipped beyond the edge and plunged downward. It seemed to explode in his face...

IT grew out of the darkness, a place of familiar beauty. The light came slowly like the first faint tracings of dawn, etching the gentle slopes, the intricate, clustered outline of the forest.

Marc looked around at Toffee who was sitting beside him on the rise of the knoll. In the glowing half-light she was beautiful beyond words.

"I ought to break your thick skull," she said. "Will you never learn to pick up those huge feet of yours?"

"Huh?" Marc said.

"Tripping over that damned cord just when we'd gotten away from them all. Big-footed oaf."

"Oh, golly, that's right," Marc said. "We're back in the valley."

"You're darned tootin' we're back in the valley," Toffee said fretfully. "And that means it's all over. No high-life, no snaky-dressed, and no..."

"There wouldn't have been any of that anyway," Marc put in hastily. "It's just as well."

"Don't be too sure," Toffee said with a sidelong glance. "All I needed was a few more minutes and..."

"What happened to your gadget?" Marc asked, changing the subject.

Toffee picked up the instrument from the grass beside her and shook it. It made a loose rattling sound.

"I broke it when I hit you over the head with it." She tossed it away from her and it rolled down the slope and out of view. "It's served its purpose." She turned to Marc. "That is if you'll just stop making people want to kill you."

"I feel all dented and scratched," Marc said. "But I guess I'm all right."

"You'd feel more dented and scratched if I'd gotten ahold of you," Toffee said. "For instance..."

Suddenly she twined her arms around his neck and kissed him. For a moment Marc felt that he must have gotten mixed up with a metal clamp.

"Gee whiz!" he said as she released him.

"That's just the beginning," Toffee said. "I like to ease into these things. After that..." She stopped as the light of the valley began to dwindle. "Oh, damn!"

Marc looked around at the valley in the rapidly diminishing light. A small pang of regret flickered deep inside him. He felt himself drifting off into the growing darkness.

"Goodbye, Toffee," he whispered. "Goodbye."

He felt the light caress of her hand on his cheek.

"So long, you lovely old reprobate," Toffee said. "Don't you dare forget me…"

And then the darkness was complete and Toffee and the valley were gone in a swirling haze.

CHAPTER FIFTEEN

MARC stirred and there was a small thud beside him. He opened his eyes and looked around; the thud had been the lamp rolling off his chest. He forced himself to sit up.

There was just enough light from a small skylight above to see that Toffee was no longer there. He hadn't really expected that she would be. He shook his head briefly to clear it. The memory of Julie and the others in the courtroom came to him.

He had to get out of there. He had to get home. He could wait there and explain things to Julie—somehow—when she returned. He got to his feet and gazed bleakly down the long, unshapely stretch of his own bare legs.

It wouldn't do to go wandering around on the streets like that. Remembering that he had noticed a closet when he'd first entered the room, he made his way to it now and opened the door.

The only thing in the closet was the judge's discarded black robe. Marc regarded it for a moment but nonetheless took it off the hanger. It was much better than nothing. He slipped the robe on and crossed to the door leading into the hallway.

He unlocked the door and opened it. The hallway was deserted. It led toward the back of the building and outside. Marc quitted the room and quickly traced the hall to a set of outdoor steps leading down to a parking area. He started forward, then drew back as a figure appeared from around the far corner and made for one of the cars. Then suddenly he stopped as he realized that the figure was Julie and she was on her way to their blue convertible.

"Julie…?" he called.

Julie, whirling about, caught sight of him and screamed at the top of her lungs. Having expressed herself thusly she leaped for the car, tore the door open and threw herself inside. Then, slamming the door and snapping the catch, she started fumbling feverishly in her bag for the keys.

Marc hastened down the steps and across the lot. He banged on the car door.

"Julie!" he cried. "Listen to me! I can explain about the girl. She was only helping me trap the congressman. She's gone now. Julie, are you listening?"

Julie paused in her frenzied gropings and looked out at him. She lowered the window just a crack with an unnerved hand.

"Beat it, you—you apparition!" she quavered. "I can't see you, I really can't! So it's no good you're pretending you're there. You're not, and I know it. Go away!"

"Apparition?" Marc said. "I'm no apparition. Julie, it's me—Marc!"

Julie's gaze steadied a trifle. "You're sure?" she asked. "You're really there?"

"Of course I am. Let me in the car, please, dear."

SHE hesitated, but in the end she opened the door, reached out gingerly and touched him. Then, with a smile of reassurance, she slid over to make room for him beside her.

"Oh, Marc!" she cried. "I'm so glad it's you. I thought I saw you just sort of fade away in there and...I guess I've been out of my mind with worry."

Marc reached out an arm and drew her close to him. "It's all right, dear," he said. "It's all over now."

"But the doctors said you had to be operated on. They said you were dying."

"Oh, that," Marc said hedging. "Well—that was just a gag, a trick to make the congressman expose himself. Where are the doctors now?"

"Asleep," Julie said.

"Asleep?"

"Yes. It seems that one of them got excited and spilled a big can of chloroform on all three of them. They looked very relaxed when I left."

"Probably needed the rest," Marc said. "They seemed quite energetic." He patted her shoulder. "So do we. Shall we go home?"

Julie nodded. Marc started the car.

"Marc…?"

"Yes, dear?"

"About that girl, the one with red hair. That was very silly of me, wasn't it?"

"Silly?" Marc asked.

"The way I got it into my head that there was something between you two. That was silly, wasn't it?"

"Very silly," Marc said. "I don't know how you thought of such a thing." He turned and smiled. "But I forgive you."

Julie moved closer. "Thank you, dear," she murmured. "You're very kind and understanding. Besides, if I'd just stopped to think about it I'd have realized she wasn't the kind you'd ever give a second thought."

Marc backed up the car and drove off the lot. "Of course not, dear," he said. A smile played at the corner of his lips as he gazed off into the distance. "Never a second thought…"

*   *   *

George approached through the mists, his ectoplasm disheveled and drooping. As he moved toward the sentry station it was apparent that here was a shade in low spirits.

"George Pillsworth, spiritual part of the mortal Marc Pillsworth reporting in from leave," he announced listlessly.

The sentry, a gross specter of the lower sort, jutted his head out of the opening. "Hot dawg!" he said. "Wait'll the Council gets a load of you!"

George looked up wearily. "What do you mean by that?" he asked.

"Just after you took off, word came through that Pillsworth was as hail and hearty as health biscuits. They've been waiting up for you ever since. Boy, are you in for a welcome!"

George shrugged and sighed heavily. "Back to the Moaning Chorus, I suppose?" he said.

"You know it, brother," the sentry nodded, and leaning forward he swung the gates open in a wide gesture. "Pass on, George Pillsworth, spiritual part of the mortal Marc Pillsworth. Come and get it, kid."

George drifted disconsolately through the gates and toward the Council Chambers which loomed large and formidable through the swirling mists ahead. Slowly, softly he began to hum to himself, a tune of great melancholy and gentle discord. He paused, hummed the tune again.

"Not bad," he mused, "not bad at all. With a little arranging it might go over big."

Humming the tune again, he resumed toward the chambers. He shrugged, dusted his ectoplasm and smoothed it down.

Now that he stopped to think about it he was sort of relieved to be back. Certainly the Moaning Chorus couldn't be any more exhausting than what he'd just gone through on Earth. And, coming right down to it, those humans down there were beginning to get a little spooky lately....

THE END

If you've enjoyed this book, you will not want to miss these terrific titles…

ARMCHAIR SCI-FI & HORROR DOUBLE NOVELS, $12.95 each

D-31   **A HOAX IN TIME** by Keith Laumer
             INSIDE EARTH by Poul Anderson

D-32   **TERROR STATION** by Dwight V. Swain
             THE WEAPON FROM ETERNITY by Dwight V. Swain

D-33   **THE SHIP FROM INFINITY** by Edmond Hamilton
             TAKEOFF by C. M. Kornbluth

D-34   **THE METAL DOOM** by David H. Keller
             TWELVE TIMES ZERO by Howard Browne

D-35   **HUNTERS OUT OF SPACE** by Joseph Kelleam
             INVASION FROM THE DEEP by Paul W. Fairman,

D-36   **THE BEES OF DEATH** by Robert Moore Williams
             A PLAGUE OF PYTHONS by Frederick Pohl

D-37   **THE LORDS OF QUARMALL** by Fritz Leiber and Harry Fischer
             BEACON TO ELSEWHERE by James H. Schmitz

D-38   **BEYOND PLUTO** by John S. Campbell
             ARTERY OF FIRE by Thomas N. Scortia

D-39   **SPECIAL DELIVERY** by Kris Neville
             NO TIME FOR TOFFEE by Charles F. Meyers

D-40   **JUNGLE IN THE SKY** by Milton Lesser
             RECALLED TO LIFE by Robert Silverberg

ARMCHAIR SCIENCE FICTION CLASSICS, $12.95 each

C-10   **MARS IS MY DESTINATION**
             by Frank Belknap Long

C-11   **SPACE PLAGUE**
             by George O. Smith

C-12   **SO SHALL YE REAP**
             by Rog Phillips

ARMCHAIR SCI-FI & HORROR GEMS SERIES, $12.95 each

G-3   **SCIENCE FICTION GEMS, Vol. Two**
            James Blish and others

G-4   **HORROR GEMS, Vol. Two**
            Joseph Payne Brennan and others

If you've enjoyed this book, you will not want to miss these terrific titles...

ARMCHAIR SCI-FI & HORROR DOUBLE NOVELS, $12.95 each

D-1   **THE GALAXY RAIDERS** by William P. McGivern
         SPACE STATION #1 by Frank Belknap Long

D-2   **THE PROGRAMMED PEOPLE** by Jack Sharkey
         SLAVES OF THE CRYSTAL BRAIN by William Carter Sawtelle

D-3   **YOU'RE ALL ALONE** by Fritz Leiber
         THE LIQUID MAN by Bernard C. Gilford

D-4   **CITADEL OF THE STAR LORDS** by Edmond Hamilton
         VOYAGE TO ETERNITY by Milton Lesser

D-5   **IRON MEN OF VENUS** by Don Wilcox
         THE MAN WITH ABSOLUTE MOTION by Noel Loomis

D-6   **WHO SOWS THE WIND...** by Rog Phillips
         THE PUZZLE PLANET by Robert A. W. Lowndes

D-7   **PLANET OF DREAD** by Murray Leinster
         TWICE UPON A TIME by Charles L. Fontenay

D-8   **THE TERROR OUT OF SPACE** by Dwight V. Swain
         QUEST OF THE GOLDEN APE by Ivar Jorgensen and Adam Chase

D-9   **SECRET OF MARRACOTT DEEP** by Henry Slesar
         PAWN OF THE BLACK FLEET by Mark Clifton.

D-10   **BEYOND THE RINGS OF SATURN** by Robert Moore Williams
         A MAN OBSESSED by Alan E. Nourse

ARMCHAIR SCIENCE FICTION CLASSICS, $12.95 each

C-1   **THE GREEN MAN**
         by Harold M. Sherman

C-2   **A TRACE OF MEMORY**
         By Keith Laumer

C-3   **INTO PLUTONIAN DEPTHS**
         by Stanton A. Coblentz

ARMCHAIR MASTERS OF SCIENCE FICTION SERIES, $16.95 each

M-1   **MASTERS OF SCIENCE FICTION, Vol. One**
         Bryce Walton: "Dark of the Moon" and other tales

M-2   **MASTERS OF SCIENCE FICTION, Vol. Two**
         Jerome Bixby: "One Way Street" and other tales

If you've enjoyed this book, you will not want to miss these terrific titles…

ARMCHAIR SCI-FI & HORROR DOUBLE NOVELS, $12.95 each

D-11   **PERIL OF THE STARMEN** by Kris Neville
        THE FORGOTTEN PLANET by Murray Leinster

D-12   **THE STAR LORD** by Boyd Ellanby
        CAPTIVES OF THE FLAME by Samuel R. Delaney

D-13   **MEN OF THE MORNING STAR** by Edmund Hamilton
        PLANET FOR PLUNDER by Hal Clement and Sam Merwin, Jr.

D-14   **ICE CITY OF THE GORGON** by Chester S. Geier and Richard Shaver
        WHEN THE WORLD TOTTERED by Lester Del Rey

D-15   **WORLDS WITHOUT END** by Clifford D. Simak
        THE LAVENDER VINE OF DEATH by Don Wilcox

D-16   **SHADOW ON THE MOON** by Joe Gibson
        ARMAGEDDON EARTH by Geoff St. Reynard

D-17   **THE GIRL WHO LOVED DEATH** by Paul W. Fairman
        SLAVE PLANET by Laurence M. Janifer

D-18   **SECOND CHANCE** by J. F. Bone
        MISSION TO A DISTANT STAR by Frank Belknap Long

D-19   **THE SYNDIC** by C. M. Kornbluth
        FLIGHT TO FOREVER by Poul Anderson

D-20   **SOMEWHERE I'LL FIND YOU** by Milton Lesser
        THE TIME ARMADA by Fox B. Holden

ARMCHAIR SCIENCE FICTION CLASSICS, $12.95 each

C-4   **CORPUS EARTHLING**
        by Louis Charbonneau

C-5   **THE TIME DISSOLVER**
        by Jerry Sohl

C-6   **WEST OF THE SUN**
        by Edgar Pangborn

ARMCHAIR SCI-FI HORROR GEMS SERIES, $12.95 each

G-1   **SCIENCE FICTION GEMS, Vol. One**
        Isaac Asimov and others

G-2   **HORROR GEMS, Vol. One**
        Carl Jacobi and others

If you've enjoyed this book, you will not want to miss these terrific titles…

ARMCHAIR SCI-FI, & HORROR DOUBLE NOVELS, $12.95 each

D-21   **EMPIRE OF EVIL** by Robert Arnette
           THE SIGN OF THE TIGER by Alan E. Nourse & J. A. Meyer

D-22   **OPERATION SQUARE PEG** by Frank Belknap Long
           ENCHANTRESS OF VENUS by Leigh Brackett

D-23   **THE LIFE WATCH** by Lester Del Rey
           CREATURES OF THE ABYSS by Murray Leinster

D-24   **LEGION OF LAZARUS** by Edmond Hamilton
           STAR HUNTER by Andre Norton

D-25   **EMPIRE OF WOMEN** by John Fletcher
           ONE OF OUR CITIES IS MISSING by Irving Cox

D-26   **THE WRONG SIDE OF PARADISE** by Raymond F. Jones
           THE INVOLUNTARY IMMORTALS by Rog Phillips

D-27   **EARTH QUARTER** by Damon Knight
           ENVOY TO NEW WORLDS by Keith Laumer

D-28   **SLAVES TO THE METAL HORDE** by Milton Lesser
           HUNTERS OUT OF TIME by Joseph E. Kelleam

D-29   **RX JUPITER SAVE US** by Ward Moore
           BEWARE THE USURPERS by Geoff St. Reynard

D-30   **SECRET OF THE SERPENT** by Don Wilcox
           CRUSADE ACROSS THE VOID by Dwight V. Swain

ARMCHAIR SCIENCE FICTION CLASSICS, $12.95 each

C-7   **THE SHAVER MYSTERY, pt. 1**
       by Richard S. Shaver

C-8   **THE SHAVER MYSTERY, pt. 2**
       by Richard S. Shaver

C-9   **MURDER IN SPACE** by David V. Reed
       by David V. Reed

ARMCHAIR MASTERS OF SCIENCE FICTION SERIES, $16.95 each

M-3   **MASTERS OF SCIENCE FICTION, Vol. Three**
       Robert Sheckley, "The Perfect Woman" and other tales

M-4   **MASTERS OF SCIENCE FICTION, Vol. Four**
       Mack Reynolds, "Stowaway" and other tales